MAYHEM IN THE CATSKILLS

MAYHEM IN THE CATSKILLS
is a Ward Eastman mystery
and a sequel to
MURDER IN THE CATSKILLS

Mayhem in the Catskills

Norman J. Van Valkenburgh

PURPLE MOUNTAIN PRESS
Fleischmanns, New York

Mayhem in the Catskills
First Edition
1994

Published by
PURPLE MOUNTAIN PRESS, LTD.
1060 Main Street, P.O. Box 309,
Fleischmanns, New York 12430-0378
914-254-4062
914-254-4476 (fax)
Purple@catskill.net
http://www.catskill.net/purple

Library of Congress Cataloging-in-Publication Data

Van Valkenburgh, Norman J. (Norman James), 1930-
    Mayhem in the Catskills / Norman J. Van Valkenburgh. -- 1st ed.
        p.   cm.
    Sequel to: Murder in the Catskills.
    ISBN 0-935796-60-6 (hc) -- ISBN 0-935796-59-2 (pbk.)
    1. Catskill Mountain Region (N.Y.)--Fiction.   I. Title.
PS3572.A5445M38   1994
813'.54--dc20
                                                        94-45461
                                                        CIP

Manufactured in the United States of America.

5 4 3 2

To the memory of
Edward G. West
Land Surveyor, mentor, and friend,
who had character and looked for it
in stone walls, tree blazes, piles
of stones, and in people, too.

Prologue
Wednesday, October 21, 1964

THE GUNSHOTS became echoes as the sound of them reverberated from wall to wall inside the small cabin. One would probably have done the job, but two made it a sure thing; the shooter didn't do things halfway. The bullets went true to their mark. Two holes appeared side by side, no more than an inch apart, in The Baron's chest. The echoes ceased and the silence was punctuated by the thin curl of smoke that spiraled upward from the barrel of the handgun.

The Baron clutched at his chest with both hands as if to hold in the blood that appeared on the front of his shirt. It didn't do any good; the blood seeped through between his fingers. He looked down at it with an unbelievable look. His body crumpled and then fell, face down, on the floor at the feet of the shooter. The shooter stood there, silently, and watched to see if The Baron would make any further move. He didn't. When a thin trickle of blood began to trail across the floor, the shooter grinned—a grin of satisfaction followed by a soft chuckle that grew into a laugh.

The shooter walked to the desk in the corner of the room under the big window that looked out to the clearing in front of the cabin. The shooter put the gun on the desk and picked up the sheet of paper that lay there. Scrawled across the front of it, in a broad, sweeping hand, the words read; "Will be at the cabin at 9:00 AM. Want to see you about this matter of extreme importance." The shooter again laughed, this time at the words "extreme importance" at the end of the note. Indeed. And, The Baron had come, promptly at 9:00 AM; he couldn't ignore the summons.

The shooter walked across the room to the fireplace at the back wall of the cabin. The shooter had built a fire there early in the day against the chill of the October morning. The sheet of paper didn't take long to burn. The edges of it curled as the flames caught. It turned black, then red, as the fire consumed it. The shooter laughed again, stirred the fire and scattered the paper into bits, mixing them with the firewood, coals, and ashes. It was destroyed completely; it might never have existed.

The shooter didn't again glance at the body. It was time to move on. It had been comfortable waiting there in the cabin beside the open fire and the brisk fall air would now seem colder than it really was. The sun was well up—as up as it got in late October—but it didn't send down a lot of heat. The shooter picked up the parka that lay where it had been carelessly thrown on the wood box next to the fireplace and put it on. Once the fire had begun to blaze high in the morning darkness, it hadn't been needed any longer. The handgun fit easily into the deep pocket on the inside of the parka and that's where it went.

The shooter stepped out the door, snapped the lock on the inside doorknob, and pulled it shut. The Baron's pickup truck sat in front of the cabin at the end of the road that wound up the valley and through the woods, crossing and recrossing the stream on its way. A trail ran beyond the end of the road and followed along the stream, which became smaller and smaller the higher up the clove it went, it would finally end—or begin, depending on one's point of view— against the upper rim of the mountain at a minute spring that seeped from beneath a ledge of rocks. The shooter took the trail and, with the sure and measured steps of an experienced hiker, climbed higher and higher, without stopping, up the steepening slopes.

About halfway up, a copse of spruce trees grew some distance off the trail and the shooter moved across to them. The trees, their branches thick and close to the ground, clustered around the lower side of a large rock. The shooter got down on hands and knees and wormed under the tree limbs into a small clearing next to the rock. The sleeping bag had been rolled up in the uncertain light of the early morning and stuffed with other supplies into the knapsack that sat there. The shooter took the handgun from the inside pocket of the parka, pushed it far back under the small hollow under the rock, and filled the opening with stones and dirt and twigs scraped from the ground nearby.

That done, the shooter backed out under the spruce limbs, pulling the knapsack along. It didn't really have that much in it, after all, one doesn't need many supplies or much gear to get through one night out in the open, even in the cold of the fall season high on one of the remote peaks of the Catskill Mountains. But the pack was lighter now, being less the food eaten the night before. It hung easily on the shooter's back and added to the impression of a hiker out on an overnight. It would be important to look like one belonged in case another hiker showed up along the trail. But no other hikers came along, so no one saw from which direction the shooter came as the trail was regained at the crest of the ridge.

It was quiet back in the cabin and remained so for a long time. The fire in the fireplace snapped and crackled as it burned down. Only coals remained when the body laying on the floor moved slightly. The Baron wasn't dead after all, but the minutes he had left on this earth were few and he knew it. He tried to raise himself on his elbows, but couldn't. The blood had stopped running from the bullet holes, but it was still damp and sticky on The Baron's shirt and on the bare floor beneath him. He turned his head as if listening for a sound. Had he heard someone in back of the cabin? He managed to twist around so he could see the window set in the back wall on the far side of the fireplace. It was covered by a window shade—the windows in the front wall were enclosed by heavy drapes, but the shooter had opened these wide long before The Baron came that morning. Was that another sound? Was someone there by the back window?

The Baron edged himself, ever so slowly, across the floor toward the window. The blood started to trickle again from the holes in his chest and a thin line of it traced the track he followed as he crawled. It seemed to take forever, but he finally reached the window. It was quiet outside, perhaps nothing had been there after all. Yet, The Baron painfully raised himself and stretched his arm up for the shade. He missed it the first time and lay still, flat on the floor, as if gathering strength for another attempt, which he knew would be the last. In time, he did try again, grasping for the shade and reaching it. He collapsed to the floor, pulling on the shade. It ripped from the roller that held it and fell on top of him. It had been pulled out full length over the window and that's the way it came down, it fell so that it covered The Baron like a blanket. Actually, it was more of a shroud because The Baron didn't move again.

But nothing stirred outside the now uncovered window. If something had been there, the noise of the falling window shade had frightened it away. It was quiet for a long time after that. The fire died out completely, its life also ended, and the red of the glowing coals faded. No more smoke circled up the chimney. The pickup truck sat in front of the cabin. The chipmunk that lived under the cabin came out, chattered at the truck because it didn't belong there, and skittered back under the cabin. The sun drifted across the southern sky.

Finally, some sounds did come from down the road; that is, if anyone had been around to hear them. It seemed like people talking and they were. The sounds settled down into words, with a curse now and then, as the people got closer. It was the survey crew that had been working on and off for over a year determining the boundaries of the vast property. The Baron had told the land surveyor he wasn't in any rush as long as he knew the job would be finished eventually. Today the crew was running a traverse up the road so it could be accurately plotted on the final map of the overall property. This particular traverse would end at the cabin and the cabin itself would be tied in with angles and distances and the sides of it measured so that it, too, could be plotted on the map.

The first person to come in sight around the last bend in the road below the cabin was Ward Eastman, the land surveyor. He was striding along purposefully, swinging his double-bitted cruiser's ax, and glancing back impatiently now and then. He saw the pickup truck and momentarily wondered about it before turning his attention back to what he was there for, which didn't include the truck. He stepped to the side of the road at the outside edge of the bend and grasped a two-inch maple sapling that grew there. Standing in back of the sapling, he looked down the road. Then, moving around to the opposite side, he looked up at the cabin. Evidently all was in order, because he shook his head in apparent satisfaction, took a step back, and, with a few swift and sure swings of the ax, chopped the sapling down so that the top of the remaining stump was about three feet high. This he fashioned into a point with his ax and tapped a tack in at the top of the point, yelling to someone yet unseen, "Turn on it."

He moved on toward the cabin mumbling something that sounded like "why can't they keep up?"

Ward Eastman was a land surveyor from the past. Now in his early sixties, he had been swinging an ax out in front of a survey crew for over forty years. In the early days, no one could keep up with him, but now the mountains were higher and steeper and all those half his age and younger who followed him in the woods had no trouble keeping up. In fact, they could have passed him if they had wanted to, but it was more fun to let Ward hold the lead just so they could hear him grumble now and then about "that damn younger generation anyway, can't keep up." He knew they could and they knew he knew, but it didn't matter; they played their parts and each was the better for it.

In time, one young lad appeared around the bend in the road. Steve was dragging a three-hundred-foot steel measuring tape. He reached the transit station, pulled the tape taut and held one end of it next to the tack at the top of the maple stump. He hollered, "Point two six" and an answering holler came from out of sight back down the road, "Two sixty-six; two sixty-six point two six." Steve waited by the transit station for a few minutes and then walked on up the road toward the cabin, where Ward had driven a stake in the ground in the open area next to the truck. By this time, Bruce had come around the bend, carrying the transit over his shoulder. He set the transit solidly, centered it over the tack, and wrote some figures and notes in the yellow-covered notebook he carried in the pouch on his belt. The uninitiated would have wondered what each of the three were doing and why, but would have been enthralled watching them. Each knew exactly what the other was doing, when it would be done, and what was then expected of him. They were precise in what they did and an efficient crew; they covered a lot of ground in a short time.

It was getting late in the day and they had a long hike back down the road to where their own truck was parked at the gate at the end of the public road. Unless, that is, The Baron (Ward knew it was his pickup truck parked in front of the cabin) was about and offered them a ride out. It would have to be an offer though, Ward wasn't going to ask. He had once asked The Baron for keys to the various gates scattered around the estate, reasoning that if they could open them and drive the woods roads to the distant parts of the property, it would save the crew considerable time and effort. Ward got his first taste of The Baron's unpredictability in his reply, "No, damn it all.

I'm paying you good money to do a survey for me; if you can't do it on your own two feet, I'll sure as hell find somebody who can." Yes sir, The Baron was one of a kind all right; no wonder the rest of the family and all those who worked for him went silently about their business when he was around. So, Ward and the crew would walk out before asking for a ride and that was that.

The final angles turned and the last distances recorded, all that remained was to measure the dimensions of the cabin. Bruce had drawn a sketch of it in his notebook and waited, pencil in hand, for the lengths to be called out to him. Ward took the end of a fifty-foot cloth tape that he had carried in his pack and pulled it along the front of the cabin while Steve waited with the reel on which it was wound at the far corner of the cabin. Ward looked in the big window at the left of the front door as he walked by and saw that the cabin consisted of a single room with a kitchen at one end, bunks at the other end, and a living-room area in the middle in front of a big fireplace. He did see something on the floor under the back window, but gave it no more than a glance. He held the zero-end of the tape at the corner of the cabin while Steve pulled it tight and read off "Forty-four even" at his corner. Bruce wrote "44.0" on the front line of the sketch of the cabin in his notebook. Ward continued on around the corner, pulling the tape behind him, and held the zero on the back corner. Steve moved up to the front corner where Ward had been, reeled in the excess tape, pulled it tight, and read off "Twenty-four point five." Bruce penciled in "24.5" feet for the width of the cabin.

Ward started across the back of the cabin and stopped at the back window. The sun, shining through the big undraped windows on the front, brightened the inside. This was the kitchen end of the cabin; he could see a refrigerator and a stove, a table and chairs, and a line of bookcases and cupboards against the side wall. Then he noticed a streak of red across the floor leading up to what seemed like a sprawled body covered by a small sheet just under the window. It was a body. He could see the feet and the legs from the knees down stretching out from under the sheet or whatever it was.

Thinking back a couple of years to his discovery of Jerry Ford's skeleton on the big rock, Ward Eastman could only shake his head. "Jesus Christ" he muttered, "not another one." But it was.

1.
The Early Years

THE BORDEN FAMILY were a curious bunch. Well, not really. It was just that the local folks were curious about them; therefore, the Bordens were curious. In the end, the Bordens were probably no more curious than the locals, who liked to call themselves natives. Some even debated whether or not the Bordens were natives. The standard (set, of course, by the locals) was that one wasn't a native unless he was of, at least, the fourth of the family's generations to have lived in the valley. Some pointed out that the present generation was the fifth counting the first Borden, who came into the valley with the railroad back in the 1870s. That certainly was a major factor until those on the other side of the argument said that since most of the Bordens didn't live year-round in the valley, whatever generation they were didn't matter. And that certainly was a point, too. What difference it made one way or the other was outside the discussion anyway. The Bordens were curious and that's all there was to that, which, of course, brought the whole debate back to where it had started.

The true natives were the Indians, but nobody still alive in the valley remembered any of them being around. Yet, they must have been there once; if not, why was the main stream flowing down the valley called Indian Brook?

The story was that when the first settlers began to move upstream in the late 1700s, they found an old Indian living in a ramshackle cabin up near the headwaters. He turned out to be a recluse who didn't much care for people white, red, or otherwise, and kept to himself while tending his stony vegetable patch, snaring rabbits, and fishing in the stream to eke out a meager existence. Some said he'd been left behind by the others of his tribe when they went north to Canada because he was so ornery and they thought they would be better off without him. In time, he died and the settlers burned his shack and buried him next to a large hemlock tree nearby. No one was quite sure now just where the grave site was, but most thought it was about where the Borden's hunting cabin now stood.

It was Thomas Borden who built the first cabin and the main lodge on down the stream on a rocky bluff overlooking the valley. Well, he didn't build the lodge himself; he brought in an architect from the city and he, in turn, brought in a number of craftsmen and they did the actual construction. Some of the local farmers were hired on too, but they were used mostly to haul in stones and to cut the timber used to construct the massive lodge. Three stories high it went. The first story was entirely of stone and the top two were made of big logs that were cut 'way up the valley and drawn to the site by the farmers. They couldn't understand why it was anyone needed a three-story building, but the pay was good and, if Thomas Borden needed three stories, they'd keep hauling logs as long as he said so.

When he had the small stream dammed up and dredged out to create a five-acre pond in back of the lodge, that was just a bit much thought most of the farmers. Why anybody needed a pond when Indian Brook kept running all year just down the hill was beyond them. Still, the pay was good and they'd haul all the rocks it took to build any sized dam Thomas Borden wanted.

At this late date, no one was sure which had come first, the railroad or Thomas Borden. They did know he and the railroad were one and the same and that it (the railroad) had run from Kingston up along the Esopus Creek, over Pine Hill, turned north at Arkville (then called Dean's Corners), and ran on into Grand Gorge and beyond to eventually reach Oneonta. They thought Borden had something to do with steamboats on the Hudson River and the railroad seemed to be an extension of that transportation system. Put together, the two systems were moneymakers and that's what the Bordens were best at, making money and spending it.

Some checking into the deed records might have answered the chicken or egg question. Who or what was first? The railroad or Thomas Borden? Perhaps the best answer was, both. The documents down at the County Clerk's Office in Kingston dated the deed to the land on which the lodge and the pond were located as running to Thomas Borden in 1869. At that time, construction of the railroad was well underway, having begun the year before on the docks at Rondout, the Hudson River harbor at Kingston. It was not until the summer of 1871 that the first train topped Highmount above Pine Hill. Ten years later, the name of the depot there was changed to Grand Hotel Station in recognition of the aptly-named, massive, resort structure that had been built near the site by Thomas Borden and his partners.

Both the lodge and the pond were completed in 1870, but it was the following year before the Bordens took up summer residence there. They might have come in by train, but the maiden run over the new line didn't occur until September. No one doubts, record proof or not, that they returned to their winter home in Kingston that fall by railroad. Would Thomas Borden have allowed his family to travel any other way?

As the years passed, Thomas Borden himself came to spend less and less time at the mountain lodge he had so carefully planned and then watched over while it was being built. He found his diverse business interests demanded closer attention than he could give them from the remoteness of the Catskills' retreat. However, his wife, their children and their families thought the summers the best time of the year. They came earlier and earlier to the mountains and reluctantly left only when cold winds began to blow and falling leaves warned that snow was soon to follow to cover the ground and ice would still the waters of the pond.

Recognizing the strong attachment that Orson, his oldest son, had for the lodge and the valley, Thomas Borden deeded the Catskill Mountains' land over to him in 1890. Orson was forty-five at the time, had made his own fortune (based largely on his father's advice) and was willing to spend it for what he wanted. It was during Orson's tenure of ownership that the first seeds of discontent were sown that would explode in gunshots decades later.

Orson Borden (he was named for the doctor who had delivered him and was a good friend of his father's) was obsessed with the ownership of land and set a goal—or so it seemed—to acquire all the land in the valley. He found himself in competition with the State, which was then just beginning a land acquisition program to add to the Catskill Forest Preserve that had been created by law in 1885.

The State's interest was in the high mountain land overlooking the valley rather than in the bottom land making up the farms that followed, one after another, up and along Indian Brook. Still, Orson Borden was not willing to share "his valley," as he had come to call it, with the State or with any other owner. In the end, things came out nearly even. The State acquired about half of the mountain land and Orson bought the other half. Both probably paid more for it than they should have. Of course, the farmers who owned the land didn't complain; worse things could have happened than being caught in the middle of a bidding war for land they thought wasn't worth the amount of taxes they had to pay on it every year.

Then, Orson Borden went after the bottom land or, more particularly, the waters and the bed of Indian Brook and a strip of land along each bank of the stream. Orson had developed a liking—more like a fixation, some said—for fishing when he was a youth. He hadn't known Izaak Walton, angler extraordinaire and the patron saint of fishing, because he was of a time much earlier than the ascendancy of the Bordens. But he did know Theodore Gordon, which was much the same thing, and fished with him over on the Neversink.

Theodore Gordon had a fortunate background similar to that of Orson Borden; that is, he was part of a prosperous family. The connection between the two came after Gordon had found his way from Pittsburgh, where he had been born in 1854, to the valley of the Neversink River, just one range of mountains away from Indian Brook. Gordon was slight of build and in ill health most of his life, apparently from tuberculosis. But he found solace on the trout stream and, it seems, a boost in vitality from the cool waters and the pure air, because he lived to the good age of sixty. He remained a bachelor, living as a semi-recluse in his haven on the Neversink, and devoted his life to the improvement of those waters and fishing in them.

Some say Theodore Gordon tied the very first dry fly. He didn't. The dry fly originated in England with one Frederic Halford being its principal advocate. In 1890, the same year Orson Borden succeeded to the land in the Indian Brook valley, Gordon wrote to Halford inquiring about this new weapon in the perennial battle of wits between the fisherman and the wily trout. In reply, Halford sent a set of his dry flies and, from then on, Gordon tied his own, including the famous Quill Gordon, and the legend was begun. It was after Gordon introduced Orson Borden to the beauty and grace of fly fishing that he (Orson, that is) decided he would create his own private trout water.

Once the ownership of the mountain land was settled, Orson set out after the nine miles of Indian Brook that lay between a large tract of land he had acquired up against the slopes of Twin and Hawk mountains and its confluence with the East Branch of the Delaware down near Milltown at the foot of the valley. The flow of the Indian began in a spring high up on Twin Mountain and the land Orson had purchased held all the rills and small runs that made up the headwaters.

Orson had confidence he would succeed and his first purchase in the project was a farm set back in a hollow that branched off the main valley. There he constructed a fish hatchery and then all he needed was a stream flow in which to plant the fingerlings produced by his hatchery. The farmers along Indian Brook watched all this with satisfaction, rubbed their hands together, mentally raised the price they would ask when Orson arrived at their door, and imagined the fine fishing they would have once Orson got his project together.

But Orson Borden was a shrewd bargainer. He knew the farmers and, especially, the farmers' wives, who were interested in security and a place to live out their old age. A few of the valley farms Orson was able to buy outright. Generally, these weren't particularly suited to farming anyway and the farmers were sick and tired of trying to scrape out a living from the steep hillsides and stony ground. This was the topsoil that well fit the description "two stones for every dirt" for which this part of the Catskills was known. Price was not a sticking point with these farmers; they were looking for a quick way off the farm and out of the valley.

On other farms, Orson struck a deal that allowed the farmer and his wife to continue using the land for the remainder of their lives and full title didn't pass to him (or to his descendents, in some cases) until their death. In the interim, however, Orson paid the taxes on the property and had exclusive rights to Indian Brook as it flowed through the farm. Orson bought the entire of some farms except for a few acres including the farmhouse and outbuildings. The understanding here was that Orson (or, again, his descendents) would have the first right to acquire the excepted parcel if and when it was to be sold out of the farmer's family. In other cases, Orson was able to acquire only the stream and a strip of land (usually fifty or one hundred feet wide) along each bank. In those instances, the farmer retained the right to water his livestock in the stream and to cross it to get from one part of the farm to the other.

All this land and stream buying occupied Orson Borden from 1890 to 1910, when he suddenly died. Some said it was from apoplexy brought on by his frustration at not being able to own the whole valley of the Indian. Whatever, he had made a valiant effort; at his death, he owned all but about one mile of the stream, this being spread out in scattered parcels up and down the valley. And the fishing was great. The farmers who owned those parts of the stream that Orson didn't, never wanted for sport or, especially, for a supply of trout for the supper table. They weren't as particular as Orson about how they caught them either. That dry-fly fishing wasn't for them. Some used worms for bait, some used nets, and others simply felt around under rocks with their hands and scooped Orson's trout up on the bank. The trout were Orson's, nobody disputed that. But if they wandered out of his water and into theirs; well, the farmers couldn't just pick them up and send them back.

Orson Borden's vast holdings weren't confined to just the lands and waters in the valley of the Indian and his will shared out his estate equally among his children. All except the Catskills' property, that is. That was treated separately, as well it should be, considering the time, effort, and money he had devoted to it. He didn't want the next generation or the next to be able to undo what he had done. So he left the Indian Brook valley—lands, waters, buildings, trout, and everything else to his oldest son, but in a custodian-type ownership. The oldest son—his name was Frederick, who had been born in 1871—could use the property and treat it as his own as long as he lived. He could add to it, but he couldn't subtract from it. And when he died, it was to pass to his oldest son and so on and so on and so on, from generation to generation.

At the time of the writing of his will, Orson knew, of course, he had an oldest son and that his oldest son had an oldest son, because his grandson, Jackson, had been born in 1895. Just what would happen to the property in the next generation, or the next, if no oldest son came along or if one oldest son died before his father or in case of, well, all sorts of things, none of the locals could figure out. But it was all there in the will. Not surprisingly, Orson had everything thought out and written down so that no female descendent would ever have more than a peripheral say in what happened to or with the Catskills' land. Every eventuality had been taken care of. It was spelled out completely, but remained hidden amongst the whereases, the whatfors, and the henceforths, written down by some lawyer in the obscure way they usually did things so that another lawyer was needed to figure out what the first one really meant. But, then, that's what lawyers were for; perpetuating the profession, some say.

Frederick Borden was in sharp contrast to his father. Where Orson tolerated the other residents of the valley simply because they were there and he legally couldn't do anything about it (although he certainly would have liked to), Frederick made it a point to know each of them, who was married to whom, which child belonged to which couple, and what their likes and dislikes were. While Orson had talked down to everyone, even to those of his own family, Frederick greeted and treated everyone as an equal. He even stopped in at the little general store and post office at the foot of the valley just to visit now and then. He went to church whenever he was at the lodge of a Sunday and sat in the back just like the local folks did instead of laying claim to a pew down front where no one ever sat. Orson Borden was always referred to as Mr. Borden (he was, to be sure, called lots of other names, but not in mixed company), even after he was dead. But most people got to calling Frederick by that inevitable shortened version, Fred, even though that wasn't his name.

Because, you see, his real name was Georg Friedrich Hendel Borden, but nobody in the valley knew that and probably wouldn't have made the connection anyway. Somewhere along the way, Orson had become bewitched by Handel's compositions—he played them continuously on the grand piano that sat in the library next to the garden window; not well, but they were recognizable.

Handel's life was a bit inconsistent and maybe that's why Orson was attracted to his works. He was German, born in Halle in 1685, and named Georg Friedrich. His father intended that he become a lawyer, but young Georg secretly taught himself how to play the harpsichord and began to compose pieces for it. He went to London in 1710 and spent most of the rest of his life there writing one Italian opera after another, nearly twenty oratorios, countless other compositions, and, of course, his masterwork, The Messiah. In London, he spelled his name George Frideric Handel although he still pronounced his last name Hendel, as it was spelled in the German.

Handel (or Hendel, take your pick) lost his sight in 1752, but continued to compose and play the organ. He died in 1759, at the age of 74, and was buried at Westminster Abbey. Handel never married and was not known to have fallen in love. That was somewhat similar to Orson Borden; while he was married, those who knew him were sure he had never fallen in love.

It came as no surprise that when Orson's first son was born (his first child was a daughter, Heaven forbid, but she was quickly relegated to the care of a governess with orders that she was to be kept quiet and out of sight as much as possible), he was named after the German composer. He always called his son Friedrich, pronouncing the last syllable with the guttural sound demanded by the spoken German. Orson cringed whenever he heard anyone call him Fred. The family didn't dare, of course, but the local folks soon caught on and did it mostly because they knew how much it irritated Orson.

Frederick (or Friedrich, whichever) didn't care what name they used. If they were comfortable calling him Fred, well, so was he. His friendliness and the fair and honest way he treated the landowners in the valley paid off in the end. It took him almost twenty years, beginning just after Orson's death in 1910, but in the end, Frederick bought all the remaining stretches of Indian Brook that remained outside the Borden ownership. He wasn't much of a fisherman himself, but he realized what an asset the stream was and hired a stream manager to see that it was maintained in a quality condition and stocked with a native strain of trout. He instituted a system whereby any—and only—residents of the valley could get a permit to fish various sections, or beats, of the stream as assigned by the stream manager. The permits didn't cost anything, but the holders of them could fish only with flies, either wet or dry, and if they didn't abide by that restriction, chances were they wouldn't get a permit the following year. In time, the local residents developed the reputation of being among the best fly fishermen and fly tiers in the State, rivaling even those over on the Neversink and the Beaverkill. It was a far cry from Orson Borden's exclusive domain, indeed.

Even after Frederick's success in acquiring the remaining land along the stream, a number of farms and smaller lots and homes in the valley remained in other private ownerships. That was in keeping with Frederick's thinking anyway. He knew the land up and down the valley needed to be used and the fields kept open if the whole thing was to retain the pastoral image everyone wanted, the Bordens and the local folks alike. However, those other landowners also knew that if they wanted to sell all or part of their property, Fred was the one to approach first because he always paid more than anyone else would.

The next generation was another story yet. Jackson Borden cared nothing for the Catskills—hated mountains, in fact—didn't like to fish, and didn't want a lot of people around. He dreaded summers when he was growing up because he knew he would be carted off to the mountains as soon as the boarding school where he spent the rest of the year closed for the semester. It was like being sent off to purgatory or placed in solitary confinement. Nothing but birds singing and trees for weeks on end, he said, and who cared for that other than his father and those country bumpkins down the road who probably didn't even know what lay over the next mountain.

But Jackson Borden knew what lay over a lot of mountains; he also knew what lay over the ocean and how to get there. He was kin to his grandfather, no doubt about that. He liked things German and enjoyed the music of Handel as much as Orson. As he grew into his early teens, Orson took him on a tour of the Continent and he fell in love with the charm and antiquity of Old Heidelberg. It was there he wanted to go for his education he told his grandfather and Orson arranged that he would. He was fifteen when Orson died and the will provided the wherewithal and the instructions whereby Jackson Borden was to be dispatched to Germany when the time came, under the care of a guardian, of course, to seek his education and his place in the world.

What he found was something else. Differing from Orson, Jackson Borden fell in love. Just a couple of blocks away from the imposing house the guardian had rented with Orson's money was a bakery. The counter clerk in the morning when Jackson stopped in for strudel to munch on while on his way to the private school where he was enrolled, was the buxom, blonde (pigtails and all), smiling daughter of the baker. As time went on, it took longer and longer for Jackson to select his morning pastry. He enquired of Brunnhilde Barron (that was her name) about the filling of each roll and pondered long before deciding which one he wanted for that day. Fortunately, the feeling was mutual, as the saying goes, and Hilde looked forward to Jackson's coming each morning as much as he did.

It didn't take long for Jackson's instructors to notice a shortening of his attention span with the proof being in the low grading he attained in the first evaluation period. The guardian was called in and he, in turn, dispatched a telegram off to Frederick, who booked passage on the next boat. It took much persuasion—the vital point raised by Frederick was that control of the funding for Jackson's schooling and his stay in Germany rested with him until Jackson was twenty-one. Things settled down then and Jackson became the bright scholar everyone thought he was capable of being.

He was, of course, still deeply in love with Hilde and she with him, but both knew they had to be patient and wait until they were "of age." They almost made it, but Hilde became pregnant when they were each only twenty. A marriage was hastily planned; it was held without Frederick, who was prevented from coming by the chaos in Europe that had upset traveling schedules, but he reluctantly gave his blessing by telegram.

But happiness was short-lived. The child was born—it was a boy, the first-born son so necessary in the Borden family—but Hilde died in the process. Jackson's grief was overwhelming, but he retained enough presence of mind to name the child after his first love and, he said, the only one he ever would have.

Barron Borden—The Baron of later years—was born in 1915. He would die forty-nine years later in a hunting cabin half a world away.

Heidelberg held no attraction for Jackson Borden with Hilde gone. Also, the events of the war had completely disrupted Germany, and the rest of Europe, for that matter. After the Battle of the Marne in September of 1914, the Western Front settled into a trench warfare some miles short of Paris. To Jackson, that city seemed to offer a refuge from his grief, so he summarily dismissed his guardian (or, keeper, as he had come to think of him), packed up his baby son—over the vehement protest of Hilde's parents—and left what had once been the place of his dreams. Indeed, the dream had come true, but now it was dashed and nothing else seemed to matter.

Travel was not easy in those days of stagnant war, but money proffered in the right places and placed in the right hands worked wonders then, as always. In time and after a number of detours, the two of them, father and son, ultimately arrived at their destination, a bit disheveled, but otherwise none the worse for the experience.

Jackson fell into a Bohemian sort of existence, taking up residence in a garret in Montparnasse and mixing with the other outcasts, wanderers, dreamers, and expatriates who made up the colony on the left bank of the Seine. As Barron grew, he was left pretty much to himself, finding his own way up and down the streets and fighting his own battles. Before he was ten, he had learned the ways of the back alleys and how to contrive an existence by stealth, wile, and cunning. The gendarmerie never quite caught him in any wrong-doing—not that they didn't try—but Barron Borden was always one block, one stall, or one alley ahead of them. He had friends among the gypsy-types who skirted the fringes of the Paris underworld and they were ever ready to give him a safe haven when he needed it.

All this kind of upbringing didn't say much for Jackson Borden; it was obvious to everyone that he had no interest in being a father and no intention of filling that role in life. After the war, Frederick made a couple of trips to Paris each year in an attempt to move Jackson out of the doldrums and into a productive way of living. Failing that, Frederick wanted to take Barron back to the States and provide him with the schooling and upbringing befitting a Borden. But Jackson would have none of it. Barron Borden was his son, he told his father, and he belonged with him. And so Frederick would depart, to return in six months or so with the same mission and again meet with the same result.

In time, however, Jackson's grief was healed or, at least, was suppressed. He began to take an interest in what was happening around him and in the people who had been watching out for Barron while he had cut himself off in a sort of existentialism. He fell in love again. Well, it wasn't really love, it was more of an attraction to a poet (or, at least, that's how she styled herself) who lived in another loft across the rooftops.

Jessie Hewitt had come from the heartland, somewhere out in the plains southwest of Chicago. She had migrated to Paris in the early 1920s seeking kindred spirits with understanding who would not look down their noses at her unconventional ways like people back in the tall-corn country did. She had talent enough to be published now and then, her crowning achievement was a slim volume entitled "Thoughts of a Dreamer."

She was a match for Jackson Borden, all their friends thought, in more ways than one. They were matched in the sense that one was as dreamy and otherworldly as the other. On the other hand, Jessie still retained some of the conventionality that characterized the Midwest (although she strongly denied that she did); just enough to turn Jackson's mind in the direction of the need to settle down and put his life in order. They took to visiting each other by a scramble over the roof between their garrets. This soon turned into a more permanent arrangement and, finally, they gave up one garret and moved their few belongings into the other. It was a crowded existence, but they, including Barron, thrived in the closeness.

Frederick, however, was of another mind, when, on his next visit, he found the three of them crammed together in the single loft room. It was no life for a small boy, he insisted; they should get married, move into a proper place, and give him a home he could depend upon. To Frederick's surprise, that's just what they did. They were married the next week, with Frederick and Barron at their side, in an open field outside Paris surrounded by a number of unconcerned cows that merely continued their browsing while the ceremony went on.

That marked the transition. They bought a farm out in the French countryside, moved in, and started to raise a family. Jackson took to managing the farm, just as a country gentleman should; Jessie managed the home, just as a country gentlewoman should. The couple they hired on to do the work of the place found them easy to work for; that is, they never got in the way once instructions for the day had been given.

The family they had decided to raise came quickly. Lincoln, never called anything other than Linc, was born the next year. Nicholas, inevitably tagged Nicky, was born in 1927, a year later. Jackson, Jr., fortunately called Jack and not Junior, was born in 1930. Genevieve, or Jen, was born in 1932 and Mildred (named after Jessie's mother) was born in 1934. Mildred was not a name that easily suggested any nickname other than Millie, but no matter, one was found anyway. She was so small at birth (just under four pounds) that Linc said she looked like a mouse. That was all that was needed and, ever after, Mildred was known as The Mouse.

But all was not positive; a discontent in this now seemingly happy family still remained.

2.
1925-1942

THE PROBLEM in the idyllic setting of the gentleman's farm in the countryside was Barron Borden. It was, perhaps, ironic that Jackson Borden, who had once eschewed everything rural, was now fully at ease in those surroundings and his son was the malcontent. It wasn't Barron's fault; after all, he had received little or no guidance in his formative years. He had, instead, joined with other forgotten waifs as they foraged for acceptance by others. The move to the farm should have been just the thing for him; it should have provided a solid base from which to bring order to a confused existence. However, it didn't work out that way. He was, paraphrasing the words of Service's poem, a part of the "race of [boys] that don't fit in." His milieu was back in the streets and alleys of Paris and he yearned to be there.

His father didn't help matters. One would have expected him to look upon Barron with added affection being, as he was, the living reminder of his first and only true love. Instead, he shunned Barron and gave his love to the new round of children as they came along, one after another.

At the time of the move to the farm, Barron was eleven. He had had only minor schooling up to that point and lacked in manners and an understanding of the other social graces. Fortunately, his father (more likely than not, it was Jessie who brought it to his attention) recognized those deficiencies and Barron was sent to the Catholic school located just next door. In addition, he was put in the charge of a private tutor for the rest of the time who instructed him about how to live with people. Barron was an exceptional student; it seemed as if he wanted to learn as much as possible as soon as possible so he could recreate his own way of life.

As the younger offspring came along in the Jackson Borden family, Barron became more and more alienated from his father. Jackson doted on them and the age difference between them and Barron was a gap too large to be easily bridged. Here, however, Barron was the one to make matters worse. Somewhere along the line, Barron had learned about the terms of old Orson's will and how it devised the Catskills' land.

It was from Frederick that this knowledge came. He still visited a couple of times each year and, if Barron had a friend in the family, it was his grandfather. The two of them took long walks through the fields and along the hedgerows of the countryside around the farm. It was then that Frederick told Barron about the high hills and deep valleys, the clear waters and deep winter snows, the craggy mountain tops, and the tall hemlocks and maples and silvery birches that covered the ridges and slopes of those Catskill Mountains so far away. One day it would all be his, Frederick said, because he was the oldest son of the oldest son.

Frederick still asked Jackson at least once during each visit to let Barron go home with him for a short time so he could show him what the other world was all about. But Jackson, still exhibiting the stubborn streak that had been passed down from old Orson, continued to demur and withhold his approval.

In disgust or, maybe, in retaliation, Barron took out his frustration on his half brothers. Since he was the oldest son and since his great-grandfather had said he was to be in charge of them (well, that did stretch it a bit), he told them they had to do what he said. Linc fell in with it all; at this very young age, he lacked in gumption and fortitude and was a willing victim for anyone shrewd enough to realize it. If nothing else, Barron was shrewd and it wasn't long before Linc was doing all his own farm chores and most of Barron's. Barron took the easy and pleasant jobs, like exercising the horses, but when it came to mucking out the stables, he said that was Linc's responsibility even though the manure fork was bigger than he was.

In Nicky's case, the result was different. He, it appeared, got all his own backbone and Linc's as well. It was he who started calling his half brother, The Baron. After all, if he was going to act like one, trying to install some sort of feudal system with serfs and lords and whatever, he should have the title that went with it. Only he was not going to be a serf for anyone, The Baron or otherwise.

As the other children came along and became old enough to have chores to do, The Baron tried to get them in line too. He succeeded with Jack, who seemed to be of a docile temperament similar to Linc's. Jen was of the other ilk and as spirited as Nicky. The Mouse was too small to be much of anything one way or another. So it was that The Baron had two servants willing to do his bidding while the other two were in constant revolt; oldest son or not, those two were not impressed. Where were Jackson and Jessie while all this was going on? Who knows? Probably off in some dream world, reading poetry or involved in some other lofty, but vague, pursuit.

Fortunately for all, The Baron grew older, more sophisticated, and more restless. He had learned all he could from tutors and the local school and the time finally came when he was allowed to choose the next step in the process of his education. No one who knew him was much surprised when he decided he would seek his calling at university in Paris.

Jessie went with him (Jackson couldn't be bothered) and arranged for his courses and a place to live. His rooms were a far cry from the crowded loft he had shared with his father and Jessie those years before. But it was not long before the old crowd located him or, maybe, it was the other way around. But he didn't neglect his studies; he just led two lives, one as a devoted scholar and the other as a prowler of the underworld. He could sip absinthe with intellectuals at sidewalk cafès or swig cheap wine from the bottle with riffraff down at the lower docks of the Seine and be accepted by each. All of which would serve him in good stead during the troubled years that loomed ahead.

And difficult and dangerous times were coming. Across the Rhine, in neighboring Germany, the Weimar Republic had been replaced by the Third Reich in 1933 and the threat of a German takeover of Europe seemed all too ominous. France, however, feared not; it would be able to withstand any attempt at invasion from the east because of its border defense, the impregnable Maginot Line.

Others were not so sure—Frederick Borden for one and Jessie for another. Between them, they convinced Jackson the time had come to send the five children off to the States and the care of Frederick's household. So it was, in the spring of 1939 that they were packed up and sent off with Frederick and a governess or two (four, actually) on the long boat trip across the Atlantic. At the time, Linc was thirteen, Nicky was twelve, Jack was nine, Jen was seven, and The Mouse was five. It was understood that Jackson and Jessie would stay on at the farm, but would leave if and when it became evident that war would engulf their countryside. And it did; all too soon.

In May of 1940, the Low Countries (Belgium, the Netherlands, and Luxembourg) fell. In early June, the miracle of Dunkirk saw over 300,000 British and French troops evacuated from the beaches in front of the advancing German forces. But Dunkirk fell in the end; the 40,000 French soldiers who had been left to defend the city could do little to halt the inevitable. The next day, June 5, the Germans crossed the Somme and attacked on a 400-mile front stretching from the Upper Rhine to Abbeville. The touted Maginot Line proved no match for the massive onslaught of German armor—it might just as well not have been there for all the good it did in slowing the oncoming tide. On June 14, Paris was occupied.

Jackson and Jessie stood in front of the farmhouse as the German army rolled by on its way to Paris. They were bypassed then, but that was not always to be the case. They stood by again as an entourage passed on the way to nearby Compiègne where, on November 11, 1918, the German Empire had signed the armistice to bring World War I to an end. It was here on the same site, in the same old railway car (that had been preserved in a museum), that Adolf Hitler had decided to accept the French agreement to the German armistice terms. It was done on June 22 and the wagon-lit was moved to Berlin, there to be put on display.

No one was better suited than The Baron to be a member of the Maquis, the French Resistance organization that fought a clandestine battle against the German occupation forces during World War II. A bridge blown here, a train derailed there, and German couriers not reaching their destinations were all signs the Maquis was carrying the fight the French Government had failed to pursue. As acts of resistance increased, names began to be connected with them. Two were prominent and always spoken together. One was The Baron and the other was that of a woman, Yvonne or Yvette, no one was certain which. It was said they were a pair in more than fighting the Germans, but that wasn't confirmed either.

While it was unlikely that all of those who were a part of the underground war could be apprehended, the Gestapo made a special effort to find and capture The Baron. Through information provided by some collaborator, the relationship between The Baron and Jackson was determined. What really happened will probably never be known. One gray afternoon, a long, dark limousine appeared at the farm and Jackson was forcibly taken away in it, crushed in the back seat between two, black-uniformed, Gestapo agents. He was never again seen alive; three days later, his beaten body was found in a ditch alongside a rural road south of Paris. Three days after that, Yvonne's (or Yvette's) body was found in the same place—in the same ditch, alongside the same rural road. Those who understood that symbolism were quick to conclude who had been the collaborator who sent the Gestapo to the farmhouse in the first place.

Just before Yvonne's (that was finally straightened out) body was found, Jessie too disappeared. However, four months later, she appeared at the door of Frederick's brownstone in New York City. She told of a harrowing journey through the south of France squeezed in the trunks of cars, buried under the hay of horse-drawn carts, and scrunched down under the seats of flat-bottomed boats as they were poled across wide marshes and slow-moving rivers. She had been hustled over the Pyrenees in nighttime dashes and through Andorra into Spain. At Barcelona, she was put aboard a tramp steamer that slowly brought her and three others out of the Mediterranean and over the dangerous waters of the Atlantic.

All those happenings taken together, some said, just showed The Baron collected from those who owed him and took care of his own. This first son of the first son was to be reckoned with.

3.
Wednesday, October 21, 1964

WARD EASTMAN peered intently through the window, fixed his eyes on the body that lay on the floor of the cabin, and watched closely for some sign of movement. But nothing moved; the body was as still as if frozen in time. When Steve asked why they were waiting, Ward motioned him to silence and listened carefully, his ear pressed against the glass of the window, for some sound from inside. The chipmunk scolded from his perch on a log back in the woods as if again wondering at the continued interruptions in this usual tranquil place he had chosen as his home.

When it became clear that looking and listening was serving no purpose, Ward called Steve and Bruce to the window, cautioned them not to touch anything, and pointed out his discovery.

"Who is it?" asked Bruce.

"Hellfire and damnation, just who do you think it is?" Ward answered disgustedly. "Here we are at The Baron's hunting cabin; The Baron's truck sits out front; The Baron passed us in that same truck this morning heading in the direction of this cabin and he didn't pass us on the way back out. I kinda think it's The Baron. I could be wrong, but I really doubt it."

Bruce and Steve both nodded in agreement; not much else they could do after that learned deduction. What Ward didn't see (but knew without seeing) were the grins on their faces; they'd been through that kind of rebuke before and found this one not unexpected.

The three of them backed away from the window. It was locked; they could see the lock on top of the lower sash was firmly set in a closed position. They walked around the cabin and checked the other windows. All were locked. Ward said they shouldn't try the doors; their hands on the knobs might destroy the fingerprints or other evidence left by whomever it was had done whatever had been done inside the cabin. That probably wouldn't make much difference anyway, he told them; once the state troopers get here, chances are that ten or twenty of them will blunder through the door before any one of them remembers to check for fingerprints. That is, he continued to speculate, if they can drive here because he was sure none of them he knew would walk this far, murder or not. If it was a murder, he went on.

"We really should get in the cabin," Steve urged. "He may still be alive. Even if he doesn't seem to be, we can't be sure until we check to see if his heart's beating or not."

In answer, Ward walked to the side of the cabin and stopped at the window between the two bunks that were inside and against that wall. It took only one swing of the double-bitted ax to smash the glass in the single pane of the lower sash. He reached in, turned the lock, and slid up the window. He brushed the shards of glass from the sill and climbed through. It was The Baron all right; Ward confirmed that once he moved aside the window shade covering the body. He checked for a pulse, but felt none and knew he wouldn't when he touched the skin of The Baron's wrist. It was cold and the fingers of the hand were stiff. The Baron was dead and had been for some time.

Ward went back to the window and told Bruce and Steve what he had found. He instructed Bruce, the fleetest of foot of the two, to get back down the road to their truck as fast as he could, find a telephone, and call the police. Ward spotted two key rings laying on the desk at the front of the cabin and handed them out to Bruce.

"Probably one of these is the keys to The Baron's truck, but we should let that stay right where it is. Maybe the other one has the key that will open the gate. Try them and, if you do get the gate open, drive our truck up here and have the troopers follow you, otherwise they'll never find us. If you can't get the gate open, tell 'em to walk. It'll do 'em good."

Ward told Steve to make a number of ever-widening circles around the cabin and to look carefully for footprints or anything out of the ordinary. However, Ward cautioned, whatever Steve found he was not to touch it. Ward then started a slow and methodical inspection of the cabin. He could see where The Baron had fallen when shot. A large patch of blood in the open area in front of the fireplace answered that question. A thin, smudged trail of red led from that spot to the back window where the body now lay. It looked like The Baron and his assailant had stood facing each other in front of the fireplace when the shooting occurred—it was a shooting, Ward saw two shell casings on the floor near the wood box. Probably right where they had been ejected, he surmised. Ward was not much on guns, so didn't know what caliber the casings were or whether they had come from a rifle or a pistol. If a pistol, it had to have been one with a slide action, he guessed. He left the two casings where they lay; someone with more knowledge about those things than he would have to sort that out.

Ward went next to the body. It seemed an odd thing for The Baron to have crawled to the small back window. The other windows in the cabin had not been covered. The two large windows in the front had drapes, but these were opened wide. The two windows set in the side walls of the cabin—one on each side—had shades like the back window, but these were raised about halfway. The back window had been the only one with the shade completely drawn. Or, at least, it must have been, otherwise The Baron couldn't have reached it from his position on the floor. However, it was the window closest to where The Baron had fallen. Maybe he had heard something or someone outside the cabin. Maybe he pulled down the shade to make a noise that would attract the attention of whomever (assuming the sound had been made by a human, that is) it was back there. Maybe the shade was the closest and the only thing The Baron could reach to make any noise at all. Maybe this! Maybe that! How did he know, Ward thought. And what was he doing poking around inside this cabin anyway? He ought to be out there on the survey line. His happiest moments were out in the woods, far from the madding crowd. Madding or maddening, to him that's what crowds were and certainly something to stay away from. Now here he was wound up in something not of his choosing. He was sure his peaceful moments would be few and far between for the next few days.

"Are you all right in there?" Steve hollered in at the open window.

Ward realized he had been talking aloud to himself; another sign of advancing senility, he thought. "Yes," he answered and went on with his examination of the cabin.

The door at the back of the cabin—between the window and the fireplace—was locked, so even if someone had tried to get in that way, they wouldn't have made it. Actually, it was barred twice. Just above the doorknob was a sliding bolt that was set and above that was a hasp secured with a padlock, which was also locked. Another quirk of The Baron's? Why have one lock when two would do the job?

Ward went across to the front of the cabin, passing between the couch and one of the two overstuffed chairs that faced the fireplace. The front door was bolted, too, although it had only one lock, a snap lock set in the doorknob. Whoever had been in the cabin and the last out—in case the whoever had been more than one person—had set the lock before closing the door. There, more than any other place that he could see, was the spot to check for fingerprints. Probably nothing would be found, Ward concluded, as cold as this October morning had been, chances are the murderer (or murderers—don't be so quick to reach conclusions, Ward admonished himself) had gloves and put them on before going out.

Ward next began to circle the one room of the cabin. The desk with a chair pulled up under it sat beneath the big window to the left of the front door. The top of it held the usual things one would expect to find on a desk; a blotter pad, a decorative jar filled with pens and pencils, a lamp—one of those green-shaded things that bankers and lawyers always seemed to have on their desks—a couple of correspondence trays, both empty; an ashtray—a big one with a pipe laying in it (so The Baron was a pipe smoker; one thing they had in common anyway, Ward thought), and—it took a minute or two for it to register—no pictures. He couldn't remember ever seeing a desk without at least one photograph of a loved one, even if it was just a cat or a dog. Well, here was one. Either The Baron didn't love anyone, or no one loved him, or both. From what he knew of The Baron, Ward guessed the last was the more likely.

A line of bookcases ran from the big window on around the corner and along the side wall to a cupboard that held dishes, pots and pans, and other such kitchen stuff. Next to the cupboard was the one window in the side wall. Ward had a fondness for books and in other circumstances would have spent a few minutes—an hour or two would have been better—browsing through the titles. However, he'd have to put that off for now or he wouldn't be done with the cabin before the troopers showed up. Still, one could learn much about a person from the books he surrounded himself with. He'd just have to come back to those bookcases.

A quick scan over the shelves did find a few old friends. There was *The Complete Sherlock Holmes* and what looked like a complete set of Robert W. Service's books of poetry. Two shelves held books by James Oliver Curwood and another was filled with Zane Grey titles. Maybe The Baron was more of a kindred spirit than Ward had thought. Too bad they hadn't been able to spend some time smoking a pipe or two in front of that fireplace and talking favorite books. Too late for that now, Ward lamented, but he couldn't imagine The Baron would ever have let him—or anyone else from what he'd heard—share that kind of closeness.

The corner past the window was the kitchen area. A stove, sink, and refrigerator with a few cupboards affixed to the walls completed that. A dining table, with five straight-backed chairs, was set in front of the cupboard, in the space back of the desk. The table was bare and the sink was empty. No coffee pot sat on the stove. Whoever had been there hadn't come for breakfast; that was obvious. And the chairs were all pulled up snug under the table; if some discussion had taken place between The Baron and the person—or persons—who had been here, it hadn't been at this table.

That brought Ward to the back window and back door again—and the body, too, of course. He stepped around it and stared at the door as if asking it to talk. And it did. It was those two locks. If they were locked and on the inside of the door; and if all of the windows were locked—also on the inside—how did the murderer (or murderers, he reminded himself) get inside?

A number of possibilities existed. They (or he, or she) could have come with The Baron, but they (or he, or she) didn't, because The Baron had been alone in the pickup truck when he drove past the survey crew. The front door could have been unlocked, but that seemed unlikely given the fact of the two locks on the inside of the back door and that all the windows were securely fastened. He (or she, or they) could have met The Baron outside and they all came in together. If so, where had she (or they, or he) come from? Not up the road or they (or he, or she) would have passed the survey crew unless, that is, it was before the crew started work that morning. He (or she, or they) could have had a duplicate key, but that also seemed unlikely, given The Baron's penchant for possessiveness; he would not have allowed anyone else to have access to his personal retreat here deep in the woods.

It was all speculation at this point, Ward realized. He had far too little to go on to come up with any reliable answer. Still, it was a curious thing how someone other than The Baron had gotten into the cabin.

Mindful not to step near the trail of blood, Ward moved over to the fireplace. He knelt on the polished flagstone hearth and reached in over the pile of ashes in the grate. He could feel a warmth on the palm of his hand as he brought it closer to the grate. Carefully, so as not to disturb the ashes, he felt in back of the grate and at the sides as well. Yes, it was warm. Only a few coals were left, so the fire had burned down some time ago. That raised another curious question. Who had built the fire? The Baron or the other person (or persons)? And when? Before the shooting or after? Before made more sense than after; it had been a cold night and hadn't warmed much until early afternoon.

So, whoever was first to the cabin would probably have built a fire in the fireplace (it was the only source of heat Ward could see, other than the kitchen stove, which was gas) to get warm. Whatever the answer to the other imponderables, a fire had been burning in the fireplace some time that morning and not in the afternoon, otherwise, more coals would remain at the bottom of the pile of ashes. The fire had been a good one, because the wood box was far from full.

Beyond the wood box and behind the second of the overstuffed chairs, the corner of the building was partitioned off to enclose a small room. It was a bathroom containing a sink, a shower stall, and a toilet, Ward found as he opened the door to it. A small window was set high in the back wall above the toilet. Ward hadn't been able to see if it was locked when they circled the cabin; it was too high above the ground. It would have been too difficult to reach and climb through anyway. He looked now and saw that it was locked, just like all of the others.

The two bunks—singles, not double-deckers—were against the side wall with the now-broken window between them. The front corner of the room was walled in, too, but much smaller that the bathroom, to form a closet. Between the large window on the right front of the cabin and the door, another bookcase sat against the wall.

That completed the circuit of the room, a cursory circuit, to be sure. If Ward Eastman was to find anything that would help answer the main question of who had shot The Baron, he would need more time than he had now. Probably he never would have that time because the police would soon be here and he knew then his access to the inside of the cabin would be limited. Well, they could have it all to themselves as far as he was concerned. The outside was his domain and, if any clues of substance were to be found, that's where they'd be. Whoever had come to the cabin and gone from it had to travel through the woods—no one had come up or gone down the road that day other than The Baron. Of that Ward was certain.

Before climbing back through the broken window, Ward looked around the room once again. He had missed something; a nagging feeling told him that. He hadn't looked that thoroughly, he knew; that was up to the police, not a land surveyor who just happened to be there at the right (or, maybe, the wrong) time. He hadn't looked in the drawers of the desk, or behind the books on the shelves, or under the kitchen sink, but he felt such a detailed search wouldn't have revealed much beyond what he had already learned, which was pitifully little at that. Still, something was missing.

He looked over the room again; everything seemed to be in its place, even the pictures on the walls hung straight. They were mostly the kind of outdoor scenes one might expect to find in a hunting cabin. That was it; if this was a hunting cabin, where were the guns? None hung on the wall or in the usual spot over the fireplace—no gun rack was in sight. In fact, none would have fit anywhere on the walls or over the fireplace. And no gun cabinet was there either. Of course, that suggested that whoever had done the shooting had brought the weapon. That implied two further points; the first being the shooting had probably been planned—premeditated was the legal term, he thought. The other point—Ward had to stretch the facts a bit to reach it—was that the murderer (or murderers) probably knew no guns were in the cabin and that's why one had been carried along. If that were true, and it did seem to be a reasonable conclusion, then the murderer (one of them, at least) was familiar with the cabin. And that narrowed down the list of suspects.

"Damnation!" swore Ward Eastman as he climbed through the window. None of what had happened here was his business anyway.

That's what the police were for even though he didn't have much faith in them. He made up his mind then and there that he wouldn't let himself get involved. After his experience with the Jerry Ford murder a couple of years ago, he knew he didn't need another one to upset his regular schedule. Once was enough.

Ward saw Steve sitting on a rock in back of the cabin. "Did you find anything?" Ward asked.

"Yes and no," Steve answered. "No, I didn't find anything out of the ordinary and, yes, I did find two trails that lead on up the mountain. The first is a short one and runs along the brook to a small reservoir just below a spring. That's the water supply. You can see where the pipeline—it's buried—runs down here to the back of the cabin. The other trail goes southeasterly on up the hollow and looks to be heading for the saddle between Indian and Twin."

"Did you see any sign that anyone went up either trail today?"

"No," continued Steve, "but the ground was frozen this morning and didn't really begin to thaw until noontime, so I don't think any footprints would have been left. I didn't walk on either trail. I kept back in the woods along the edges of them so I wouldn't destroy any signs that might be there. Do you think they could use bloodhounds to track someone who might have gone up the trail?"

"I doubt it," Ward speculated. "They have to have a scent to start with and I don't know how they'd get that. I didn't find anything in the cabin that didn't belong there, so it looks like the murderer carried off everything he or she came with. All except two shell casings, that is."

By this time the sun had gone down. October afternoons in the mountains didn't last long. Ward sat on the rock and reached for his pipe. He filled it and carefully tamped down the moist tobacco. He struck one of the wooden matches he always carried (always, unless he forgot to put some in his pocket, which was becoming more often than he cared to say) and brought the flame to the tobacco, savoring the sweet, enjoyable taste of it. He made sure the first few puffs of smoke drifted past Steve's face. Steve was one of those who thought smoking was bad for one's health and Ward was always letting him know that he didn't really care. He was old enough to do what he wanted and wasn't interested whether or not others approved. He'd smoked a pipe since he was twenty; here he was at sixty-four and wasn't any the worse for wear. Steve snorted; Ward laughed and so did Steve. Although he wouldn't admit it, Steve thought the smoke from Ward's pipe smelled good and didn't mind at all when it blew in his direction.

In a short while, they heard the sound of the truck on down the road and then saw the flash of headlights through the trees. The light of day was fast fading; it was dusk."

Here comes Bruce," Ward said. "I wonder what he's brought with him."

4.
The War Years

"IT WAS THE BEST OF TIMES, it was the worst of times,..."
When Charles Dickens wrote those words to begin *A Tale of Two Cities*, he might have looked into a crystal ball and seen those years yet to come in the 1940s when the whole world would find itself embroiled in war.

The "war years" as they came to be known by later historians and by those who lived through them were, indeed, of those two extremes. For those who were in the midst of destruction and suffering not of their choosing and for those afar off who sent their sons and, yes, their daughters too, to the distant places where death was dealt out, it was "the worst of times." However, for those who, for whatever reason, stayed behind and provided the base of support for those doing the actual fighting, it was "the best of times."

For those at home—"the home front," it was called—those years were a time of togetherness, a time when everyone pulled together for a common cause; it was a time such as the country had never seen before, and never would again. Everyone was touched by the war, some more than others, of course, but all experienced its effect. Rationing hit everyone; most learned to live with less except those who profited in the black market—some always are ready, no matter what the circumstance, to seek gain at the expense of those who play the game as it should be played. People young and old (age was no barrier in those times of stress) participated in scrap drives. People who had never hoed a hill of beans, planted a victory garden and took pictures of it to send to their sons overseas. People who had never seen an airplane close up manned observation posts and scanned the skies watching for enemy 'planes. Farmers who could plow a straight furrow for miles if need be, learned how to march (although no one was quite sure why) in the local gym, but still walked as if they had one foot in that furrow. Women who had never knitted before turned out warm sweaters and scarves for those who stood watch on decks of ships during long, cold nights at sea. And so it was in the valley of the Indian.

In the spring following the sneak attack on Pearl Harbor, Frederick moved Jessie and the five children out of the city and took them to the mountains. For all intents and purposes, he had become their father; with Jackson gone and Jessie not quite able to overcome her loss, the children needed a firm hand and his was the only one available. Although he was into his seventies by then, some of their youth provided vigor to his aging body and he became their friend and, in those pursuits their mother forbade, their co-conspirator. It was he who helped Nicky build the glider in the garage out back of the barn. It was he who had the land cleared and the ski run and ski jump built in the deep hollow a mile up the road (where Jessie never went) so that Linc could train in preparation for enlisting in the Tenth Mountain Division. It was he who took Jen to the spring hop in town so she could dance with that towheaded boy she thought was a dreamboat. What he had not been able to accomplish as Jackson's father, Frederick more than made up with his grandchildren, but time was growing short.

The mountain lodge was the permanent residence for the Bordens during the war years. All the boys (and Jen) were, of course, sent to boarding school when they became of age. Linc, who had dreams of being a general, was enrolled in a military academy out near Syracuse.

Nicky (as he grew older, he tried to convince everyone to call him Nick, but Nicky it remained) wanted to fly, but no prep school devoted to flying could be found. Instead, he was sent to a small institution in New Hampshire that specialized in mathematics and the sciences with the idea being that training in those disciplines would provide a solid foundation for later studies in aerodynamics. Nicky wondered about the necessity of all that when all he really wanted was to be in the cockpit of a B-17 Flying Fortress, or a P-40 Warhawk, or a P-39 Airacobra, or a whatever as long as he could get it off the ground.

As much as Nicky wanted to fly, Jack wanted to float. When Nicky was building model airplanes, Jack was crafting four-masters and sailing them across the pond. An east-coast school was thought to be too dangerous—reports of submarine sightings were becoming common along the eastern seaboard—but, finally, a suitable school with some nautical connection was located on the shore of Lake Ontario in upper New York State.

Jen was to be a lady, so Jessie said, but she hadn't reckoned with the headstrong and independent nature of her oldest daughter. ("Takes right after her father," Frederick said, and he should know.) Whatever others might want Jen to be, Jen decided to be the opposite. It was animals, horses especially, that attracted Jen. Frederick pre-vailed on her behalf and enrolled her in a downstate school on the banks of the Hudson that majored (or so its catalog seemed to indicate) in horsemanship—or horsewomenship, because it was an all-girls school.

The Mouse was kept at home—at the lodge, that is. She was too young, too small, too fragile, too everything to be sent anywhere. A tutor was hired and The Mouse was taught all subjects proper for girls, including how to be a lady since it was becoming more and more obvious that Jen wasn't going to be one.

For all that, it was the summers and holiday vacations each looked forward to. They came in by train from all points of the compass when these interludes occurred, arriving at Grand Hotel Station at all hours (trains that ran on regular schedules were among those things the home front gave up for the duration). There they were met by Frederick and Jonathan, the chauffeur, whatever the hour of the day or night. All except Linc, that is. He walked (or skied in the winter) the six miles from the station to the lodge and, sometimes, shortened that distance by going cross-country, up and down the ridges in between. "All part of my training," he said, still in quest of his goal of becoming a part of the Tenth Mountain.

These respites from their grueling studies (well, they really weren't that bad, although the boys would have everyone believe otherwise) were, indeed, "the best of times." The boys, and Jen as well, came to know the valley of the Indian and the deep hollows, high ridges, and summits that made up the vast holdings of the Borden ownership and the adjoining State land better than any other member of their family ever did, before or since. They explored it all, and in all seasons.

Jen was the loner of the bunch; at least everyone thought she was. She discovered trails where a horse could go along the ridges up and down both sides of the valley. Jessie insisted she was too young to be out on those trail rides alone. "Suppose the horse is startled by something or other and throws her? She'd never be found. Suppose a sudden thunderstorm comes up—they're common in the summertime Catskills you know—and she gets struck by lightning? Suppose and suppose and suppose," bewailed Jessie. But none of those dire things ever happened. "Even if they did," said Nicky, "Who'd miss her?" Well, they all would, everyone knew that, even Nicky.

But Jen wasn't alone much of the time. As it turned out, that towheaded boy down the valley was a bit of a horseman himself. Unbeknownst to anyone (except Jen, that is), he had been riding over the Borden lands for a couple of summers before Jen came to the lodge to live. In fact, he was the one who had routed some of the trails and cut out tree limbs here and there so horse and rider could easily pass. He and Jen had chanced to meet (no, it hadn't been planned by either of them) on top of the ridge across the valley from the lodge one clear and fine day the first summer she took to riding out on her own. She was not quite a teen-ager then, but he was, being a couple of years older. They had both come to the ridge top to enjoy the view that stretched easterly for miles—almost to the Hudson River, it seemed. Neither was shy and talk came easily to them as they sat, their legs dangling over the edge of the high cliff that provided the look out.

His name was Amos Kirk and he had always lived in the valley. He hated his name, the Amos part, that is; he could put up with Kirk. The last came from being born, he said, but Amos had been given to him and he'd just as soon give it back. But he'd been named after his grandfather and he was a grand old guy, so guess he'd go on being Amos for his sake. And then he wanted to know how come Jen was alone. After all, it was dangerous for girls to ride by themselves, didn't she know that? That brought the predictable response from Jen, although Amos didn't yet know what was predictable about her and what was not. She could take care of herself, so there. And she was probably a lot better rider that he was anyway, so there, too. Then they both laughed and a long friendship was begun. Just the same,

Amos said, it would be safer if they rode together whenever they could. Jen agreed. And they did.

During one of those summers, Nicky decided to build the glider. Well, he didn't really decide in the summer. Actually, he had decided the winter before and spent many hours—when he should have been studying—in drawing up plans for the glider and making lists of materials he would need to build it. The New Hampshire school had a good collection of books on early airplanes and flying and Nicky based his design on the plans of some of the early Wright Brothers gliders he discovered in one of the books. He scaled it down some from their models, but kept the same proportion of wing surface area to weight. Once he finalized the design, he sent a list of necessary materials off to his grandfather. Frederick immediately fell in with the plan and ordered everything. As soon as items were delivered, he stored them in the empty garage out back of the barn—all in secret, of course.

Construction of the glider took most of the summer. The design was workable, but each component had to be formed as they went along. Neither Nicky nor Frederick were particularly adept at that, so they brought in a partner. Henry, the local handyman, could build anything and he was put in charge of manufacture, although he admitted he had never before built an airplane. Hell, he'd never even seen one except those that flew overhead and they went so fast you couldn't see how they were put together. It was a grand thing when it was done and they were all proud of the results. Now, if only it would fly.

The next question was where to fly it and Linc quickly settled that. (He and Jack had been brought into the scheme early on. Once they realized something was going on out in the garage of which they weren't a part, they decided they should be and just walked in one day.)

"Why not fly it off the ski jump?" Linc suggested.

"Perfect," said Nicky.

"Can I fly it, too?" asked Jack.

"No," gruffly answered Nicky. "It's my glider and it's designed to hold only one person and that's me."

They waited for just the right time to fly it or, better put, they waited until Jessie went off on one of her weekend shopping trips to the city. They loaded the glider onto a flat-bed truck and Jonathan drove it carefully up to the jump. By now, the whole family and most of the resident help knew about the glider and it seemed that everyone had gathered to witness the maiden flight. All except The Mouse, that is; she said she just knew Nicky would get killed and she wasn't going to watch that.

Well, Nicky didn't get killed, but he darned near did. The first part of the test flight went just fine. Henry, the handyman, had added a track down the center of the jump and exaggerated the lip at the end to give the glider a better lift as it took off. Somewhere, Frederick had found a leather flying helmet, goggles and all, and Nicky looked the part of a World War I flying ace as he took his place in the glider, prone and faced forward, just the way Orville and Wilbur had done it. In fact, the tension and expectations were probably no less than they had been at Kill Devil Hill. Frederick, Linc, Jack, and Henry gave it a hardy shove and the glider was sent off down the greased track, gathering speed as it went. It was going a good clip as it lifted off the end of the jump and took to the air like a bird to the accompaniment of cheers and applause from the crowd of well-wishers below.

Nicky was a good pilot. He had spent a lot of time at the site, watching and studying the wind patterns and air currents. He had laid out a flight path in his mind and followed it perfectly. Straight out from the jump; then a bank to the left out over the trees; next a bank to the right to circle back over the clearing to catch the updraft over the jump; then another left bank and around again to a landing in the flat area at the bottom of the slope below the ski jump.

All would have gone as planned if that spruce tree up-slope from the jump had been ten feet lower and the wind hadn't died all of a sudden. No matter what he did, Nicky couldn't find the lift he needed to clear the topmost branches of the tree. The glider crashed and hung there, high in the air. Nicky was flung clear and tumbled to the ground, falling through the branches of the spruce, which, fortunately, broke his fall so that he hit bottom with less velocity than he might have. Nothing was broken—except the glider, of course—but Nicky was scratched and bleeding from head to foot. He looked worse than he was; the goggles and flying helmet had protected his eyes and head. But he had a lot of explaining to do when Jessie arrived home on Monday. Even with Frederick's help, that didn't turn out too well—about as good as the final moments of the flight of the glider, actually.

Linc and Jack were more down to earth, but height was not unknown to them. They fought the war in the mountains, building strongholds of sturdy lean-tos (well, not very sturdy; most of them fell down with the first hard rain) in secluded draws high on the hills. From these redoubts, they attacked the summits where the dreaded Nips and krauts were holed up. They always prevailed, although in every battle, the odds were overwhelmingly against them. In particular, they beat the German defenders into submission, giving no quarter to the dastardly Huns who had killed their father. Whether it was in these imaginary encounters or because of the discipline and training they received in school, they gained confidence in themselves as they grew—no longer would they be browbeaten by The Baron or by anyone else, for that matter.

Back down in the valley, once the latest skirmish had been won, they joined the local boys in various scrap drives. The purpose of each one varied depending on what was needed at that moment for the war effort. One time, scrap iron would be collected; the next time, it was aluminum; then, old car batteries, paper, or tin foil. The scrap-iron drive was especially successful. On one of their forays into the hills, Linc and Jack had discovered the tracks of an old railroad spur leading to an abandoned rock quarry. Once Frederick gave his approval to salvage the rails, all the boys worked for days dismantling the tracks and carrying them down to the highway where the road crew loaded them on the town truck and took them to the county collection center. Another time, the two of them collected over one hundred used tires and posed with them so the photographer from the weekly newspaper down in Milltown could take their picture for the front page of the next edition.

Their favorite expedition, however, was the long hike up Spruce Lake Mountain to the State fire tower. They made this an overnight trip, setting up their tent in a little clearing hidden amongst a grove of small, gnarled spruce trees. They ate their evening meal—usually a feast of hot dogs, potato chips, and sugar cookies—on the ledge out front of the clearing. They cooked the hot dogs stuck on the end of sharpened sticks held over a smoky fire and at least one hot dog always dropped off. No matter, once they retrieved it from the coals and brushed off the ashes that clung to it, they thought it tasted as good as the meal Hannah, the German cook at the lodge, had prepared the night before. This living off the land was all right they decided, and blackened hot dogs went with the territory.

They especially enjoyed visiting with Hiram Mead, the observer on the tower. ("Just call me Hypie, everyone else does," he told them.) He let them up in the cab at the top of the tower when he was on watch and they could see for miles in every direction across the ridges and valleys to far-off mountain peaks. In the hot and humid days of summer, they just knew the coolest place in the Catskills was in the cab of Hypie's tower. He took out the windows all around to let in the cool breeze of the high mountain. Once it picked up Hypie's daily record sheet and his other "official papers," as he proudly called them, and blew them out one open window. They watched as they drifted out of sight over the next ridge, riding the air currents that circled the lofty ranges.

The tower was one of the observation stations in a network that stretched up and down the eastern United States to provide a system of early warning of approaching enemy airplanes. Some were in fire towers, such as the one on Spruce Lake Mountain; in the big cities, they were on the rooftops of tall buildings; out in the country, they were in small shacks set on a ridge or hill. All of the observation stations or posts, as they came to be called, were sited in some high place that commanded a wide view of the open sky. These were manned, night and day in many cases, by local residents who were on watch for airplanes, enemy or otherwise. Every airplane that was seen, or even if only heard, had to be reported by telephone to a command center where the progress of each 'plane was plotted on a huge map as additional reports from other posts were called in. Each post had a call sign that was used to identify the source of the observer's call. The number of airplanes, their height, distance from the post, direction of flight, number of engines, and other pertinent information had to be reported by the observer.

The whole system was called the Army Air Forces Aircraft Warning Service and those who manned the posts were titled Aircraft Spotters or Observers. They were authorized to wear a bright blue armband with a circular emblem in white enclosing blue letters spelling out "U.S. Army Air Force—AWS." Wings of gold flanked the emblem and underneath it, letters of gold proclaimed the wearer to be an "OBSERVER." The Service was discontinued in May of 1944, just a week or so prior to D-Day on the Normandy beaches. All "loyal and faithful" volunteers were given a certificate testifying to their service and were transferred, so the certificate said, to membership in "the Army Air Forces Aircraft Warning Service Reserve."

Those still alive are members still of that reserve force, one supposes because it was never reactivated or officially discontinued.

Hypie was the one and only spotter at the Spruce Lake Mountain post and his call sign was Oboe 071. Linc and Jack were sure Hypie didn't know what an oboe was; he didn't know how to pronounce the word, that they knew. They always hoped an airplane would go over when they were at the tower just so they could hear Hypie begin his report. "Hello, this is Oby-Oh-Ee 071. . . ." Hypie always used three syllables to pronounce the two-syllable word. They never laughed at him—that wouldn't have been polite—but they smiled at his uniqueness and wondered what the plotter receiving the call at the command center must think about it. Not much, they decided, Hypie was probably no more rustic than a lot of other observers and he was justifiably proud of the part he was playing in winning the war for the good guys.

Linc and Jack did, however, laugh once at Hypie. After finishing their supper, they walked the short trail that led from the ledge by their camp across the ridge to the fire tower. Hypie always smoked a pipe after his supper and they liked to sit with him on the porch of the small cabin next to the fire tower where he lived during the summer. Hypie was always good for an hour or two of stories about the people—those now living and those who had passed on—of the valley and the surrounding countryside. And just as important, the smoke from Hypie's pipe kept away the mosquitoes and punkies that came with the dusk.

When they reached the cabin, Hypie was still eating at the small table by the front window. He hollered out the open door for them to "take a chair" there on the porch. Just then, seemingly out of nowhere, they heard the roar of an airplane as it came, hugging the contours of the mountain, up the valley of the Beaverkill off to the southwest. Hypie heard it too and came running out of the cabin, his binoculars in hand, just as the 'plane roared overhead about one hundred feet off the ground, passing close to the tower. One could hardly miss seeing the airplane and identifying all the main features that needed to be reported to the command center. In fact, the 'Plane was so close Linc and Jack later said they could see the color of the pilot's eyes—well, that did stretch it some, but it was close, no doubt about that.

Hypie frantically tried to focus his binoculars on the 'plane. He insisted on doing this for every airplane he spotted and for every smoke he sighted off in the distance. The binoculars were part of his "official government issue," he was proud of telling all who visited the tower and he usually carried them hanging on a leather strap around his neck. But this time the 'plane was so close and going so fast that he never did see it. It disappeared over Hawk Mountain while Hypie was still turning in all directions, the binoculars clamped to his eyes, and urgently asking, "Where is it? Where is it?" When he realized it was gone, he asked the boys if they had seen it. Of course, they had and, in fact, Linc easily identified it as a P-40.

"Well, you'd better call it in then. Since I didn't see it, I can't very well tell those people anything about it," said Hypie sadly. Linc did, being careful to identify himself to the command center as "Oby-Oh-Ee 071."

The Mouse was oblivious to the war and to most of what went on outside the closed circle of her immediate world. She was too young to fully understand what war was all about and, while she knew it had been the cause of her father's death, she had only a few memories of him. She was, in fact, much like her mother. Early on in their studies, the tutor, a retired professor from a girls' college down the Hudson River, realized that The Mouse had an interest in the classics and a leaning toward the Romantic poets. She later penned a few poems of her own and with her mother's help, sent them off to a few of the specialty magazines. No one was more surprised than Jessie when one was accepted.

It wasn't that The Mouse didn't want to be a part of the family, because she did enjoy being with Jen and the boys; when they would put up with her, that is. However, she better liked her privacy and could be seen most hours of those summer days sitting on the little balcony outside the French doors of her second-story room. She took her lessons there, studied there, read the classics there, and wrote her poems there. Sometimes, she even sat there in the rain, a bright yellow umbrella protecting her from the elements. Nicky said she was so dreamy she didn't know enough to come in out of the rain. Of course, he thought nothing himself of spending a couple of hours fly-fishing on the Indian in the rain and Linc and Jack had climbed a number of the mountains of the Catskills in the falling snow of a winter's storm.

Jen told her to pay them no attention. "They're just boys," she said. "What do they know?"

But The Mouse really was different. She knew it, but didn't much care what others thought. In that, she was a typical Borden, said her grandfather, and that didn't diminish his affection for her, nor anyone else's either.

The war finally ended in Europe when Germany surrendered unconditionally on May 7, 1945. The war in the Pacific dragged on a few more months, but, at long last, it too ended, on August 15, following the dropping of atomic bombs on two Japanese cities in the previous two weeks. Almost as if he had waited for the war to run its course, Georg Friedrich Hendel Borden, better known in the valley as Fred, died in September of 1945, quietly, in his sleep. He was seventy-four years old.

Paris had been liberated on August 25, 1944, but periodically, over the previous two years or so, Frederick and Jessie had heard from Barron and had been able to send messages to him. He was living at the farm in the countryside outside Paris when word reached him of Frederick's death. He knew about the will of his great-grandfather and the manner of succession of the Catskills' property. The lure of Paris and of France and of Europe, for that matter, had paled for him as the events of the war had unfolded across the continent. He was thirty years of age in 1945, but the war and the unsettled years of his youth had aged him. He looked—and felt, he said—ten years older than he really was. He needed a change of scenery, of surroundings, of people, of responsibilities, of place. With his grandfather and his father both dead, and with his father having been an only child, The Baron was now the oldest son of the oldest son and the time had come for him to claim his birthright.

Barron Borden arrived in the valley of the Indian in the middle of a blizzard in January of 1946 and, although no one realized it at the time, that was a harbinger of things to come. The warmth of the summers of years past was about to be replaced by the chill of winter.

"But," as the poet wrote, "Times do change and move continually."

5.
Wednesday and Thursday,
October 21 & 22, 1964

WARD EASTMAN rose from the hard seat of the rock and tapped the now-cold ashes from his pipe. He and Steve watched the headlights of the truck bob up, down, and from side to side through the trees as it banged and swerved over bumps, holes, and stones in the rough, one-lane, dirt road. "He's driving a whole lot faster than the road calls for," Ward said. "I wonder what's the hurry?"

Later Bruce told him the troopers didn't want to drive their cars up the road and asked him to bring them in the truck. "They wanted a ride and I gave them a ride," related Bruce. "I really gave 'em a ride."

As the truck braked to an abrupt halt in front of the cabin, the uniformed trooper in the passenger seat of the truck lurched forward. The wide brim of his hat hit the rearview mirror and it (the hat, not the mirror) was knocked askew to a rakish angle Ward thought certainly looked unbecoming for an officer of the law. That was only half the story, however. Both Ward and Steve noticed that one of the two troopers standing (or trying to stand) in the back of the pickup didn't have a hat. They learned later that when the truck passed under a low-hanging branch, the hat had been snapped off his head and flung into the stream. Bruce was moving the truck along at a good pace then and didn't hear the trooper calling for him to stop. When last seen, the hat was floating merrily along on the Indian, probably to be retrieved as a trophy by some local resident downstream.

"Well, Eastman, your helper here isn't a very safe driver. Don't let him loose out on the highway or we'll surely have to haul him in," complained Sergeant Burgin, as he climbed down from the cab of the truck.

Ward had known Burgin for some years and thought he was one of the best troopers around; that is, he was dedicated to his work, fair-minded, a stickler for adherence to the law, and generally well-liked by those of the community he served. Ward smiled—to himself—and answered in defense of Bruce. "I told him to hustle along and guess that's what he did."

Burgin allowed as how he certainly had hustled and then hustled some himself as he got quickly down to business. "What have you got here?" he asked. "Your young man filled me in some on the trip here; that is, what I could hear over the roar of the engine, but let's hear the whole story before we look around. Keep it short though, it's getting on toward night pretty quick."

Indeed it was. The sun had set over Spruce Lake Mountain some time ago and light had faded fast. Ward told how they first saw the body through the back window and then broke in through the side window. They hadn't tried the doors, he said, so they wouldn't destroy any fingerprints or some other evidence that might have been left on the doorknobs. Burgin nodded positively at that. Ward continued, telling about his inspection inside the cabin and Steve's look around the area outside. He knew he would have to go through all of it again in greater detail down at the police barracks in Milltown in the next day or two, so he mentioned only the critical events, keeping his story short as Burgin had asked.

By this time, all three troopers were using their flashlights. Bruce had found one too under the seat of the truck amongst the other odds and ends that always seemed to collect there. It worked, which was a surprise because the last Ward had seen it had been nearly a year ago.

"Any electricity in the cabin?" asked Burgin.

"Yes, but not the regular kind," Ward told him. "There's a generator in the shed out back. We can probably start it if you want."

"Let's not get into that; we'll have to look that over along with everything else in the light of day. Just tell Bruce to start up the truck and move it so the headlights shine through that big window in front," Burgin commanded. "We'll get along with that and the flashlights for now. Show us the window where you got inside."

Ward took them around to the side of the cabin and pointed out the broken window. Burgin leaned in and shined his flashlight around the interior before climbing through. He told King, the hatless trooper, to follow him in and instructed the other trooper to look around the front of the cabin, especially near the front door, for anything that looked like it might have some connection to the shooting or to the person who had done it. Ward watched through the open window as Burgin and King conducted their inspection. The headlights of the truck lit up the inside of the cabin about as well as the electric lights might have except grotesque shadows were pro-jected on the back wall by the furnishings that stood in the glare. This only added to the macabre scene. The body, of course, took most of their attention, but that changed when Ward directed them to the two shell casings next to the wood box.

Burgin knelt and picked up one of the casings on the end of a pencil and handed it to King, who dropped it into a small envelope. "It's a .45," he called out. Burgin marked where that casing had been and left the other one where it lay so the position of the two of them could be accurately noted when the crime-scene people from the barracks showed up in the morning.

Burgin climbed back through the window. His inspection had been preliminary, but thorough. "The lab boys will give that a real going-over tomorrow. I don't think much is going to change around here until then. Right now we should worry about getting the body out of here and down to the coroner. I called him before we left and he said he'd have Hopkins, the undertaker, send up a hearse. Now that I've been over that road, I don't think the hearse will ever make it. We might better take The Baron out in the back of the truck."

That proved to be easier said than done. Before delivering the body to the coroner, it was necessary to get it out of the cabin. Burgin had thought ahead all right. He had brought along a stretcher antici-pating that one might be needed and it was a simple matter getting it in through the open, broken window. It was army surplus and folded into a compact unit consisting of not much more than two six-foot poles strapped together. And it was no problem placing The Baron's body onto it. The trouble came when they tried to lift the opened stretcher—with the body on it—through the window. It didn't fit because the stretcher was wider than the window.

A pair of solutions were available. One was to pass the body and the folded stretcher separately through the window. All agreed this hardly seemed appropriate although Ward thought probably The Baron wouldn't care. So they opted for the other solution and that took them out the front door of the cabin. They were careful not to touch the knob on the inside of the door and, especially, the snap lock in the center of it. Burgin handed out the rings of keys (that Bruce had given him on the ride in) to the third trooper and instructed him to unlock the door without touching the knob. The stretcher, with The Baron's body on it, went easily through the opened door.

Trooper King, who was also the official photographer along with his other duties, had brought along his camera and took a number of pictures of the body, from various angles, before it was moved. Now he photographed the trail of blood, the remaining shell casing where it lay on the floor, the window shade, and the fixtures that once held it in place. Burgin, Ward, and the others could see the bright flare of the flashbulbs reflect eerily through the windows as King went about his work.

They gently slid the stretcher into the flat bed of the pickup truck and closed the tailgate. Burgin then told each of them what their next moves were to be. He, Ward, Bruce, and Steve would take the body out to the end of the town road—he really didn't care who drove the pickup, he said, as long as it wasn't Bruce. Once the driver was selected, the others would ride in back of the truck so they could steady the stretcher and the body on it as they drove over the rough road. King and the other trooper were to stay at the cabin to make sure nothing was disturbed and to be on the alert in case the killer (or killers, maybe) returned. Burgin assured those two that he would send in a relief team around midnight. He, himself, would return early in the morning bringing the crime-scene investigators.

The rough ride out the long, dirt road to the gate at the parking lot was slow and cold. Darkness enveloped them and the typical October night air of the Catskills had a touch of frost in it. Steve, who had been detailed to drive, tried to avoid the dips and holes—high hollows, Ward called them—in the road. Still, it was a bumpy trip. They held onto the stretcher so it wouldn't slide back and forth, their fingers stiff with the cold. They watched for low-hanging limbs and once heard an owl hoot from a dead maple tree next to the stream; it added to the uncanny sense of the whole journey. The headlights of the truck swept the trees and brush along the road and cast long shadows that disappeared in the gloom of the forest beyond.

It seemed a longer ride than it was, but eventually they reached the parking area at the end of the town road where Hopkins and his hearse waited. In addition, they saw two other law enforcement cars, one from the sheriff's office and the other from the local constabulary. Word sure travels fast, Burgin thought to himself and soon discovered it was Hopkins who had notified the other two officials.

"I was sure you'd want the sheriff to know what's going on, so I gave him a call after I heard from the coroner," Hopkins, a tall, gangling man who always wore a black suit no matter where he was or whatever the occasion, informed Burgin as he climbed stiffly down from the back of the pickup.

"Thanks," muttered Burgin, although not really meaning it, as he nodded to Cal Upton, the county sheriff. "Hi, Cal and, Hi, to you, too, Bill," acknowledged Burgin, turning to Bill Irwin, the local police officer.

That formality out of the way, Burgin helped Ward, Steve, and Bruce slide the stretcher out the back of the truck and into the hearse. Hopkins fretted and fussed around them watching to see they didn't scratch the hearse, which he kept polished to a high gloss. Some local wags insisted it was always shined up so brightly, Hopkins didn't have to turn the headlights on at night, the hearse itself gave off enough light to see half-a-mile in all directions. Burgin sent Hopkins on his way telling him he would come right along to the funeral home and talk to the coroner who was there waiting for the body to arrive.

Both Cal Upton and Bill Irwin understood that Burgin was in charge; they remained in the background as if waiting to see what their orders would be. It was only natural out here in the country; the county deferred to the state in most everything and the town deferred to the county. Ward never could understand just why this was so, but from his many years experience working for the state, he knew that's the way things were. He supposed it was because those who worked for New York State (himself excluded, of course) were such an overbearing bunch, they just naturally elected themselves to sit at the head of the table while consigning those from lesser units of government to the lower positions at the other end. On the other hand, Ward knew the local people usually just let the state representatives have their say and then, after they left, went ahead and did what they had planned to do in the first place.

In the case of law enforcement; however, it was a bit different. Both the sheriff and the town police knew the troopers were better trained and had more resources behind them to conduct any investigation—especially when murder was involved—so it made sense to stand back and let them run the show. In dealing with Burgin, that wasn't too difficult. He had been a local boy and was well-liked by all except those who ran afoul of the law. Although Ward had no liking for the State Police, he could get along with Burgin. Much like Sherlock Holmes thought of Inspector Lestrade, he was the best of a bad lot.

Burgin didn't disappoint them. He dispatched Upton off to Milltown to the funeral home with instructions to be present while the coroner made his examination and to not let him go until he, Burgin, got there. He directed Bill Irwin to remain at the gate and not let anyone through until he was relieved by troopers he would send back. Lastly, he turned to Ward Eastman and told him that he, Bruce, and Steve could go on home, but he wanted to talk at length with each of them sometime over the next few days. However, Ward was to be back at the cabin first thing in the morning to describe in some detail their movements and experiences before and after arriving at the cabin. Ward nodded and asked Burgin if he could talk to him confidentially about something important.

"Well, I suppose," Burgin brusquely replied. "Only make it quick, I've got to get back to the barracks and line up people for night watches and get things organized for tomorrow."

Ward winced only slightly at that retort, grasped Burgin by the shoulder and steered him down the road out of earshot of Bill Irwin. "Before things get sticky here, you should know that you're dealing with the wrong coroner, the wrong sheriff, and the wrong town policeman."

Burgin spun around quickly and glared directly at Ward—eyeball to eyeball, as the saying goes. "Just what in hell are you talking about?" he bellowed.

Obviously not yet quite beyond hearing range, Ward gently turned Burgin around and guided him a few more steps farther away. "It's a long story," Ward began, "but since you've got a lot to do, I'll make it short. The cabin where the murder took place is in Ulster County, not in Delaware County where we are now."

Burgin wrinkled his brow in disbelief and looked at Ward as if he was an escapee from the asylum down in Middletown. "How can that be? Everyone knows the county line runs over the tops of Hawk, Twin, and Spruce Lake mountains and all the others in between and along the high ridges that connect them. And the cabin is on this side of the range. Now get out of my way so I can get on with it."

Ward stood his ground and, placing one hand on each of Burgin's shoulders, held him in place. "No, it's everyone *thought* the county line followed the height of land of the range. It doesn't; it runs along a straight line that crosses the head of the valley about a quarter-of-a-mile downstream from the cabin."

Burgin, a bit quieter now, but still not convinced, demanded, "Just how do you know that?"

Now that he had Burgin's undivided attention, Ward replied less forcefully. "One of the things The Baron wanted us to find out on this survey was just where the county line was. He said years ago his grandfather had told him the two counties and the state had things all wrong and the line wasn't on top of the mountains. So we did a lot of digging around in the old laws that first set out the counties and towns and determined he was right. We ran the line through a few months back and found the monuments called for in the original descriptions. We hadn't told anyone but The Baron so far. He wanted to tell the assessor of the town of Middletown when the next tax bill came. Seems he's had some problems with high assessments—at least, he thought they were high. He was going to take the tax bill covering the land at the head of the valley into the assessor's office and tell him he'd be damned if he'd pay taxes to that town when the land wasn't theirs. Maybe he told him already. You know how The Baron is—or was—when he got his teeth into something."

Burgin just shook his head now, the look of disbelief replaced by one of confusion. "If the cabin's in Ulster County, then what town is it in?"

"The town of Hardenbergh," Ward replied.

"Oh, my gawd," Burgin exploded. "Hardenbergh doesn't even have a police unit. And the Ulster County Sheriff is way off in Kingston. That's forty miles away. They can't get here without going through Delaware County or else down through Sullivan County and then Delaware. And the same with Hardenbergh—they can't get here from there unless they go afoot over the mountain. Worse yet, the town of Hardenbergh isn't handled from my barracks. Now we'll have two state police barracks, two county sheriffs, one town police unit plus whoever shows up from Hardenbergh—probably the dog catcher. Do you realize what a mess this whole thing is going to be? The murderer will be halfway 'round the world and back again before we establish a chain of command here or even come to some agreement about who's going to be in charge. I'll vote for the dog catcher; that'll make my life easier."

Ward Eastman decided that, at the moment, silence was the only answer, so he made no reply. Bruce later said, however, he could see the smile on Ward's face even from that distance and in the uncertain light from the pickup.

The conversation was over. Burgin ended it by turning on his heel and, without another word to Ward, stomped off toward the state police car, mumbling to himself and shaking his head as he went. As he passed Bill Irwin, who stood quietly at the gate throughout it all, he gruffly said, "Wait there and don't move 'til someone with a uniform shows up."

If that was meant to be a slight to Bill, it was, because the town of Middletown didn't provide him with a uniform. He had to buy his own and he could afford only one, which was kept, cleaned and pressed, in a closet at home. Burgin made no acknowledgement that Bruce and Steve were even there, slammed the door of his car, ground the engine as he started it, and drove off, leaving a cloud of dust and flying gravel as he spun his way out of the parking lot.

"So it goes," thought Ward, but accepted it as one of the hazards of being a land surveyor. More than once—in fact, probably more than a hundred times—people got angry with him when he discovered things were different than what they expected them to be. It wasn't his fault when someone built their fence over the boundary line, or cut down the neighbor's shrubs, or paved the driveway so the outer foot or two was across the line. If people would only call in a land surveyor—one who knew what he was doing, of course, which cancelled out the majority of them—before they did anything permanent near the edges of their property. Oh well, they'd still get mad when he told them their line wasn't where they wanted it to be. "So it goes," he said again as he climbed into the pickup. As they drove off, Ward turned to wave to Bill Irwin, who, faithful to the instructions given him, hadn't moved from his stand by the gate.

It was true, they had found the original location of the county line, Ward reminded himself as the truck wound its way down the valley of Indian Brook. Considering all that had happened that day and night, it seemed darker than it was; the headlights of the truck hardly reached more than twenty feet ahead. Beyond, all was black. Neither of them spoke as they traveled along. Each was lost in his own thoughts. As if to satisfy himself that he hadn't missed something, Ward went over again in his mind the process they had followed in reaching their determination about the county line.

Ulster was one of the original counties, being created by Chapter 4 of the Laws of 1683 that divided the then Province of New York (before 1664, it had been the Province of New Amsterdam under jurisdiction of the Dutch) into counties as one of the acts of the first colonial assembly. Following the War of the Revolution and in a restating of the earlier laws, Chapter 63 of the Laws of 1788 rede-scribed the original counties, including Ulster. These laws were, however, of little importance in the upset that followed; it was Chapter 33 of the Laws of 1797 that was critical. This law, entitled, "AN ACT to erect part of the counties of Ulster and Otsego into a separate county" created (or, erected, in the legal language of the day) Delaware County.

The law, as its title implies, set out the new county of Delaware from the existing counties of Ulster and Otsego (the westerly part of Ulster being parted off and the southerly part of Otsego being parted off to form Delaware). The text of the law described Delaware County by metes and bounds that, although meager, provided suffi-cient information so the boundaries could be plotted and even fol-lowed on the ground if one was willing to spend a few months at it. The common line between Delaware and Ulster was described sim-ply, beginning on the east bank of the Delaware River and running on a northeasterly bearing "to the Mill Brook Ridge, then easterly along the height of land to a stone set up between Tunis mountain and Twin mountain, then north 62 degrees east to a stone set up on the easterly ridge of Hawk mountain, then along the height of land to the line of Great Lot 8, then. . . ." It was all very clear and not apt to be misconstrued.

However, as in the case of the texts of many of the early laws of New York State, the descriptions of the counties were repeated in laws of following years. While this may have been the system, it provided more than ample opportunity for errors to creep into the later descriptions. And that's just what happened with the metes and bounds of Delaware County when it was again set out in Chapter 39 of the Laws of 1813. Three complete lines were omitted in the 1813 law so that the description of the common line between Ulster and Delaware counties still began at the Delaware River and ran northeasterly, but the next section read ". . .to the Mill Brook Ridge, then along the height of land to the line of Great Lot 8, then. . . . "

The reference to the two stones "set up," their location, and the line between them was left out. One would think the error might have been caught when the description of Ulster County was set out further on in the 1813 law. However, since the parting off of Delaware County from Ulster and Otsego in 1797, the westerly bounds of Ulster County had been described only as "northwesterly by part of the southeasterly bounds of the county of Delaware." Both the shortened description of Ulster County and the erroneous description of Delaware County were repeated over and over in later laws.

It would seem, regardless of the error—or omission—in the 1813 law, this new description of Delaware would hold and the county line would run "along the height of land" leaving behind the stones "set up" and the line between them to rest in antiquity. However, contrary to the usual construction of these recurring laws, a short phrase was tacked onto the end of the Delaware County description in 1813 and was carried over in all the later laws. This phrase stated, simply, that Delaware County was to be "as it was erected in 1797." This subordinated all the erroneous descriptions to the original.

The error was compounded when Alexander Daniels and James Cockburn, Jr., were sent out in 1845 by "Order of the Surveyor General" for the purpose of establishing "The Division Between Ulster & Delaware County." In conducting their research prior to going into the field, they evidently turned up only the later descriptions of Delaware County and ignored the charge to look at the one written in 1797. In running the county line, once they got "to the Mill Brook Ridge "they took off along the height of land" and stayed with it until they reached "the line of Great Lot 8." And there the line stood, etched in the text of the erroneous law, in the fieldnotes of Daniels and Cockburn, in the report they wrote to the Surveyor General, on the maps that they and later cartographers drew, and on the ground as long as the trees they blazed along the way still stood. And there it would have stayed forever, if The Baron hadn't retained the one land surveyor meticulous enough to run his research back to the beginning of time or, in this case, back to 1797. And now, what had that gained him—The Baron, that is? Only that he was murdered in a part of one county that most everyone else thought was part of another.

Of course, the language of the original law did signify the intention of those state and local government officials involved in setting up the new county of Delaware. That was one thing and once Ward had that run down, he wondered if the straight line had ever been established across the head of Indian Valley. In particular, had the two stones ever been "set up?" Ward Eastman was not one to let that challenge rest for long. And a challenge it was; if someone did set those stones back in 1797; then, he was the one who could find them.

It wasn't all that simple, of course. The distance between the summits of Tunis Mountain and Twin Mountain was four miles and the height of land between them had a lot of ups and downs as well as a number of wide, relatively flat, stretches along the way. It would take some diligent searching to find a single stone "set up"—especially when no description of it had been given—in that long expanse of ground. On the other side of Indian Valley, chances for success seemed better. The easterly ridge of Hawk Mountain was not quite a mile long. It dropped southeasterly to the saddle between Hawk and another summit, which was locally called Indian Mountain, further on and the crest of this ridge was sharply defined most of the way.

It was a sweltering day in mid-July when Ward Eastman and Bruce climbed the game trail that led up along the northerly branch of Indian Brook. It headed in a large spring high up the clove and they stopped there for a rest and to splash the icy, cold water over their sweaty faces and heads. The game trail bore off across the face of Hawk Mountain, and they left it to head straight for the saddle. The saddle was broad and flat, as many of them are in the Catskills and the ridge of Hawk Mountain ran up sharply off the west of it. The saddle might have been only a mirage; they still had a long and steep way to go.

They climbed slowly, following close along the crest of the ridge. They looked carefully at each stone—and as expected in these old mountains, stones are their most noticeable product—not really knowing just what shape or size stone they were looking for or just how it would be set. It took them a long time, so slowly did they go, and as they came in sight of the flat summit of Hawk Mountain, they had nearly given up hope when they both saw it at the same time.

The birch tree wasn't that big; one wouldn't expect it to be up there so near to 3,500 feet. It wasn't tall either, the wind and the long, cold winters at that elevation stunted what trees could grow at all. It measured only about a foot in diameter, but it was old. Ward imagined that if they cut it down (which they had no intention of doing) the growth rings would be so close together they wouldn't be able to count them, even with the aid of the small magnifying glass he carried in his rucksack for just that purpose. However, it wasn't the birch tree that held their attention; it was the stone that was encased by the roots of the tree.

Once the stone had stood straight, about two feet out of the ground. Now it was tipped over at nearly a 45-degree angle, the birch tree seeming to grow out of the side of it. That wasn't how it was; however, two thick roots of the birch nearly circled the stone as they had grown around it seeking the meager soil of the mountain top. It was a squared stone—about six inches on a side—obviously cut by human hands and not formed by nature. That was what had prompted them to examine it closer; stones that uniformly shaped just didn't grow that way up in these high mountains. Only the upper foot or so of the stone was visible above the birch roots and that was crusted over with lichens. Still they could see that something was etched in it. They carefully scraped away the lichens until the etching was clear. No mistake about it, they agreed; the letter U was carved into the northeasterly face of the stone and the letter D was carved into the southwesterly face. Neither Ward nor Bruce said anything, but each grinned—satisfied grins and well-deserved ones.

They didn't rest on their success. Finding the anchor point of one end of a line nearly three miles long was great stuff, but the line was the important thing. To put that in place, they had to find the other end of it.

Fortunately, the 1797 description called for the line to run on a bearing of North 62 degrees East or, from where they were at the northeasterly end of it, South 62 degrees West. That morning Ward had corrected that bearing for the change in the magnetic declination since 1797. He set the corrected bearing on his hand compass and sent Bruce out ahead down the slope and put him on line. They continued producing the bearing in this manner down the southwesterly slope of Hawk Mountain, across Indian Brook, across the road leading to The Baron's cabin at the head of the valley, and on up the northeasterly face of the long ridge between Twin and Tunis mountains.

It was another steep, hot climb up the ridge. The sun had moved across the sky and was only a couple of hours above the western horizon. They had been so engrossed in their quest, they hadn't taken time to eat the lunches each of them carried in their rucksacks. Now it was suppertime, but still they weren't willing to stop and take time to eat.

They topped the ridge and saw they were at one of the wide, flat areas along its crest. The ground was covered with a thick, scrubby growth, mostly spruce. Off to the right, about one hundred feet away, was a boggy area about an acre in size. Even though it seemed a forlorn hope, they decided to spend the remaining daylight time giving it their best shot. Bruce threaded his way into the spruce trees, cursing as he went back and forth across the broad top of the ridge. Ward opted for the bog; it wasn't that wet at this dry time of year and, even if it was, he thought it might cool off his hot feet.

It was a short search, after all. Ward found it in the middle of the bog—he wondered why the 1797 description hadn't said that's where it was. It was a stone identical to the other one, about two feet high above the ground and six inches squared. Being in the dampness of the bog all those years, it was covered with moss about one inch thick all around. They scraped off the moss and found the carved letters—U on the east face and D on the west face.

Tired as they were—and hungry, now that the search was over—their steps had a spring to them as they climbed down the ridge to the road and hiked it back to the truck they had left at the gate that morning.

Ward told The Baron next day of their find and he directed them to run the line between the stones, blaze the trees along it, and paint the blazes with the brightest red that Ward could find. And so they did over the next couple of weeks. On the day they were finishing painting the line, The Baron met them on the road as they crossed it. He looked at the bright red paint—fire engine red, it said on the can—and laughed; a cynical laugh it was. "I can't wait to bring that damned assessor up here and show him this," he sneered. Then, he jumped in his truck and drove off down the road toward the gate, leaving Ward, Bruce, and Steve standing there and facing the long walk out.

Ward Eastman never did find any documentation explaining why the county line had been run across Indian Valley instead of around the height of land at the head. However, he guessed it might have been because the then owners of Great Lot 7 didn't want to be moved completely into the new county.

Gulian VerPlanck and Robert Livingston had acquired Great Lot 7 in the 1749 partition of the Hardenburgh Patent. On December 12 of that year, VerPlanck and Livingston released their interests in two halves of the great lot to each other, VerPlanck ending up with complete interest in the south half and Livingston getting the north half. Gulian VerPlanck died in 1751, leaving his part of the great lot to his two sons, Samuel and Gulian. Samuel conveyed his interest to his brother in 1762. Gulian was the owner in 1797 (he died in 1799), so it was he (probably) who had asked (or demanded, because he had that kind of clout) that the county line be established as it was by the 1797 law.

Ward woke with a start as Bruce brought the pickup truck to a halt in back of the Eastman house in Woodland Valley. Ward realized he had slept most of the way home and, no wonder, he thought as he looked at his watch, it was 1:30 in the morning. At least he was home; Bruce and Steve had a ways to go to get to theirs. Ward told them, "No need to come to work tomorrow, we wouldn't get much done up the valley anyway with all the police that will be wandering about getting in each other's way and ours, too."

It was raining when Ward went into the house. Not a hard rain, but one of those cold, soaking rains that come in October. And it was cold. The thermometer at the back kitchen window stood at 34 degrees. That means it's snowing up at the head of the Indian, Ward supposed. He was glad to step into the warm back kitchen, and especially glad he wasn't one of those troopers standing watch at The Baron's cabin—particularly the one with no hat.

6.
Winter, 1945-46

THE BARON'S HOMECOMING was not completely unexpected, but it was unannounced and pretty much unob-
served.It had taken him some time to dispose of Jessie's farm
outside Paris and to wind up his own business interests in the city.
Times were not easy in France in the early days after the turmoil of
cannon and gunfire and airplanes had faded into history. The destruction left behind would not fade so swiftly and neither would the
enmity felt by those who had stood firm in the face of the Nazi
aggression for those who had capitulated and aligned themselves with
Marshall Pètain and his Vichy government.

It was through his friends in the Maquis that The Baron finally
found a purchaser for the farm. Money was short—and probably
worthless anyway. In the end, the transaction was based mostly on
trust. Only a small amount of cash changed hands; the rest was in the
form of a mortgage carried by Jessie. Under its terms, a sum (not
specified) was to be paid into an account at the local bank at least three
times a year, but on no set dates. The other terms were just as
nebulous, and the task of seeing they were all satisfactorily met was
left to the president of the bank, who had been The Baron's commander in the Resistance.

It was the best deal he could get, but neither he nor Jessie seemed concerned about the uncertainty of it. The Baron just wanted done with it and to be on his way. He looked forward to he knew not quite what, but he remembered the descriptions of scenes and places and sounds his grandfather had used when telling him about the Catskills' property; the property that was now his. He pictured it as a retreat where he could rid himself of the rest of the world. He didn't intend to become just one of the idle-rich—although comfortable he now was—but he did want to leave behind the troubles of other times and places and people and enjoy the rewards of his heritage.

A telegram from Linc came soon after the one from Jessie telling him that Frederick had died. "What should we do about the Catskills' property?" Linc asked. "Do nothing with it," The Baron replied. So they didn't.

Linc and Jessie and the others closed down the lodge and the other buildings and moved back to the city. They left the caretaker and his family to run the farm complex, which was located down the hill from the lodge, and to care for the livestock. They didn't know what further instructions to give him except to watch over the rest of the property. They couldn't tell him when to expect The Baron or if he was to be expected at all. And that's the way it was left. Time had seemed to stand still ever since Frederick had moved them to the country in that first year of the war; now they and time had reached a turning point. The nights grew cold; the leaves changed color and spiraled to the ground as they too lost their hold on summer.

Once his ties to France had been severed (as severed as they could be, that is), The Baron arranged his journey home. Although he had yet to see the Catskills, he now considered them his home. It was as roundabout a trip as one might expect in those fitful days before regularity returned to the lives of those who had survived the years of war. He took a train north to Le Havre, crossed the Channel on a ferry to Southampton, and traveled into London by a train that seemed to stop every mile or so for no reason that anyone could say. There, he contrived his way on board a ship carrying soldiers returning to the States and war brides traveling to their new husbands and a society different from the one they had known although they had been told it would be as if they had never left home.

Throughout the entire journey from Paris to New York, The Baron spoke to no one other than those who had to be spoken to when buying tickets, booking passage, changing money, ordering meals, or asking directions. Overnight, it seems, he became a recluse. If not a recluse, those who traveled with him found him to be unsociable, to say the least.

It is doubtful that Jessie had any notion The Baron (or Barron, as he was known to her) would call when he arrived in New York. First of all, she didn't know when he was coming and, secondly, she suspected he might not ever come. If she had any thoughts of hearing from him, they were dashed when he passed through the city without a glance to the right or the left. He felt no urge to see his mother (well, stepmother) or his brothers and sisters (well, half brothers and half sisters), even though he hadn't seen them for years.

He took a taxi to the bus station in lower Manhatten and learned it would be a couple of hours before the next bus would leave for the mountains. It was cold; the wind whistled down the streets and the air was filled with flakes of snow being whirled about. It wasn't supposed to amount to much there in the city, he was told when he bought his ticket (one way to Milltown, he wasn't coming back), but a foot or more of the white stuff was expected on up river. He shouldn't plan on getting much farther than Kingston the ticket seller advised; if he hadn't a place to stay the night there, he should think about finding a hotel as soon as he arrived—if the bus got there at all, that is.

The bus finally did leave, only a half-hour late, after a heated discussion between the driver and the dispatcher about canceling the run altogether. The Baron took a seat near the back, next to a window. Only a few other passengers boarded and he could tell from the conversations between them that they had spent the holiday season with relatives in a southerly climate more hospitable than the cold, foreboding mountains to which they were returning. He watched the towns go by, towns he had never heard of, some in New Jersey and, then, those in New York; Goshen, Walden, New Paltz. He saw the snow piling higher along the road as they traveled north. It was eight inches deep when the bus finally pulled into the station on lower Broadway in downtown Kingston.

The downtown station was the main Kingston terminal; it was here that passengers changed buses and new drivers took them on to their destinations to the north and west. As had been predicted by the ticket agent in New York, some question arose as to whether or not the bus to Oneonta would take the road. The driver, Al Rose, had made the run in all kinds of weather, fair and foul, he said, and a little snow wasn't going to stay him from making his rounds. He was just like the mailman he told his passengers, neither snow nor sleet nor dark of night or however that went, could keep him off the road. Besides, he had this girl in Oneonta who was just counting the minutes until he pulled in. So the bus left—two hours behind schedule—heading off into a thickening snow and the dark of early evening.

Before leaving the city, the bus had another stop to make at the Crown Street Station. It was here the bus picked up the girls who worked at the uptown stores—Newberry's, Kresge's, Woolworth's, Grant's—and in the Wall Street offices. They had been waiting, and waiting, in the restaurant in the station biding their time with coffee, banana splits, and bantering with Jimmy, who left his post in the parking lot for a little warmth. The bus finally pulled in, with a toot of the horn announcing its arrival. Al swung down in the swirling snow hollering, "All aboard, hustle along, we're running late," as if the working girls didn't know it. With a wave to Jimmy, now back in the parking lot helping a distressed driver sweep the snow off her car, Al started his run.

He asked all the passengers to sit near the back, as near as possible over the back axle, to add more weight for better traction, especially when they went over the viaduct. But don't worry, Al said, the road crews all along Route 28 were the best around and they'd have the road plowed and sanded down good. In Ulster County, that is; he wasn't so sure about the stretch from Highmount down into Milltown, the Delaware County crew wasn't so reliable.

Al was right, the road was in fine shape. He pushed the bus along at regular speed determined not to fall any farther behind the schedule; after all, that girl in Oneonta wouldn't wait all night. As he drove, he kept up a running chatter, mostly to himself because the passengers were grouped in the back out of earshot. At each stop along the way, he greeted the people waiting there with a laugh telling them it was just like mushing in the Yukon. If the clerk at a stop was a young gal, Al stepped inside a few minutes, just to warm his hands over the stove, he said. They knew him and liked him at all the stops; he was a bright spot in the dreary day.

The stretch up Pine Hill was the most exciting part of the run. The road was plowed, but the increasing, strong wind blew it back almost as soon as the plow passed. Al stopped at the bottom of the hill and waited until the next plow started up. He pulled in behind it to take every advantage of the fresh track it made. The Baron and the other passengers were again positioned in the back and there they felt every swerve as the bus fishtailed its way up the steep hill. Al was a good driver though, early on in his adult life he had driven trucks loaded with logs over the narrow woods roads that wound about these hills. That was his only problem, a few people said; he sometimes drove the bus as if he was still driving a log truck.

They made it in good order though. The snowplow pulled over to the side at the top of Highmount; this was the end of their road. The Delaware County crew had the job of clearing Route 28 on down into Milltown and beyond. Al was right again, conditions did change at the county line. That didn't stop him; he blew the horn and waved to the crew on the plow as they passed it, shifted down, and bucked into the foot of snow that now covered the ground. It was an uneventful downhill run; the deepening snow slowed the bus to a crawl and Al kept it in low gear all the way into town.

Only The Baron and one other passenger, a lad of about eighteen, got off at Milltown. No one got on. After unloading the luggage of the two and dropping off the bundle of newspapers that had been sent up from Kingston, Al boarded the bus again, tooted the horn, and headed off into the blizzard, as most were now calling it. That gal in Oneonta had better appreciate what he was going through to get there, he told the few remaining passengers.

The Baron looked around the general store that also served as the bus station and housed the post office, which was walled off in the back. The store was empty except for the owner, the postal clerk behind his grated window, and a rough-looking man, who appeared to be the father of the young lad who had gotten off the bus. The Baron approached the storekeeper and asked if he knew someone he could hire to take him up Indian Brook Valley to his place there. Well, no, said the storekeeper, they didn't have any taxis in town and he couldn't think of anyone around who would want to go up the valley in weather like this. Besides that, the road probably hadn't been plowed.

Throughout this conversation, Vile DeSilva, the boy's father, stood by the door and listened to it all. He realized then who the stranger was; it must be the new Borden, come to take over what old Fred left behind. Years later, when folks hereabouts got to know The Baron, they would say it was fate that brought him and Revilo DeSilva together on that snowy, dismal evening. One was as much of a S.O.B. as the other and they were bound to hit it off.

Vile DeSilva moved away from the door and over to where The Baron and Harry Osterhoudt, the storekeeper, stood. "Reckon I could get you where you wanna go, only it'll cost you twenty bucks."

The Baron looked Vile up and down. "How do I know you can get me there?"

"Because I got a truck out there loaded down with cordwood; it's got dual wheels on the back with chains on all four wheels, and I'm drivin' it, that's how."

"Twenty dollars sounds like a lot of money for a short trip."

Vile snorted and started to move away. "If you got a better ride, go to it."

The Baron stepped closer. "You don't listen very good, do you? I didn't say twenty dollars wasn't a fair price, I said it sounded like a lot. I'll give you ten dollars before we start. If and when we get to where I want to go, I'll decide whether or not you get the other ten dollars. That decision is mine, not yours."

Harry Osterhoudt quickly checked the merchandise on display near where the two men stood and wondered if he should move it out of the way. He needn't have worried, however; Vile seemed to know he had met his match. He looked The Baron straight in the eye, seemed to want to say something, decided not to, and ended that part of the conversation with a barely perceptible nod of his head.

Although Vile had yielded that point, he hadn't backed down altogether. Osterhoudt had just begun to relax when Vile opened the next round. "I'm not just sure where you've come from, but I know where you're goin'. When we get there—which we will—you'll find the lodge has been closed down for a few months and chances are you ain't gonna find any food there or any other things you'll need. And you may find out the lodge is the only place you're gonna see for the next few days. Winter don't come one day and leave the next up here in these hills. You better have Harry there put up a box or two of supplies to take along."

That was about the longest speech Harry Osterhoudt had ever heard Vile make. He glanced at The Baron, who was quiet for a minute or two as if considering what Vile had said. Then he turned to Osterhoudt and nodded his head, which Harry took to mean that he was to put up that box or two. He hastily went back of the long counter, grabbed two large cardboard boxes, and started along the well-stocked shelves taking down a can here, a bottle there, cartons, and more cans and filled the boxes.

Vile wasn't done. "Next thing. Snow ain't somethin' you play around in, you gotta respect it along with the wind and cold that'll come tomorrow. You're not gonna last long in those henskin pants you got on or that fancy jacket or those damn slippers or whatever they are on your feet. Harry's got a good selection of fittin' kind of clothes. You better pick out some. Put 'em on and act like you belong here. The boy and I'll go out and make room for your suitcases on back of the truck. What in hell are you bringin' along in so many of them anyway?"

With that Vile headed for the door, his son following. The Baron didn't move, startled for a moment and wondering just how to take the two lectures he had just been given and, especially, how to react to the man who had delivered them. When Vile opened the door, he could see the snow was still falling; the big flakes formed a screen that hid the truck and everything else more than a few feet away. The Baron looked at the deepening snow, fingered the seam of his trousers and the sleeve of his jacket, and looked at Harry. Osterhoudt inclined his head toward the back of the store where a rack of Woolrich pants, shirts, and parkas hung and a few shelves of boots were displayed.

By the time The Baron made his selections and changed into them, Osterhoudt had taken the two boxes of food and other supplies out to the truck where Vile loaded them in the back. As The Baron reached for his wallet, Harry shook his head, "Don't worry about paying now, no one else does. Besides, I haven't figured it up yet. I'll make out a regular bill when I get time and send it up to you the end of the month. Vile will get you there. He may be an ornery cuss, but he always does what he says. Good luck."

The Baron mumbled a thanks and went out into the dark of the night. Vile and his son, whose name was Spencer ("His mother picked it out, I didn't" Vile was quick to tell anyone who asked.), were already in the cab of the truck, the motor running, headlights on, and the windshield wiper on the driver's side (the one on the passenger's side had fallen victim to a sweeping tree limb the year before and hadn't been replaced) slap, slapping, back and forth trying to keep up with the thick flakes. He climbed in the passenger side; arranged his feet amongst a pile of chains, wedges, and spikes that lay on the floor, slammed the door (Twice, it didn't catch the first time. "Slam it harder than that" Vile snapped.), and nodded his head that he was ready.

Vile did the driving as he always did when Spencer was along. ("I won't ride with him" Vile told everyone. "He goes too damn fast.")

The truck moved steadily along the main road; the plow had been through not long before, so the snow there was only a couple of inches deep. Conditions changed when they turned up the Indian Brook Road. The town crew hadn't been by for some time, if at all. They had a difficult job of it when a deep snow came because the town roads were mostly dead-ends branching off the state and county roads and were scattered from one end of the town to the other. Indian Brook Road was the farthest from the town garage and it was always the last one to get plowed. Today was no exception.

Vile swung the truck sharply to the left to hit straight on the bank of snow the state plow had pushed across the front of the Indian Brook turnoff. The truck shuddered and slowed almost to a halt. Vile downshifted through two gears and stepped hard on the accelerator; all four back wheels spun, the chains caught, and the truck broke through the snowbank onto the smooth, white track of the Indian Brook Road. Vile cranked the window down on his side and let fly a thick, brown stream of tobacco juice. "Damn state crew, anyway" he cursed to the world outside the open window.

From then on, nothing could stop or slow them down. The snow was well over a foot deep by this time, but the truck seemed built for it. Or, maybe, it was the driver. Nothing phased him. He knew where the hills were and speeded up as they approached each one; the extra momentum carried them easily over the top. He knew how sharp the corners were and took each one on the outside, crossing close to the apex of the curve, and ending up in the outside lane, all of which expanded the degree of the curve and lessened the chance of sliding off it. It was a quick trip; Vile didn't slow down for anything, he only accelerated.

The Baron was glad of two things. First, that the windshield wiper on his side was broken so he couldn't see where they were going or what tree they had just missed when the truck slued around some of the turns in the road. Second, that Spencer wasn't driving if he really was, as Vile had said, the faster driver of the two. The ride didn't bother Spencer though, he fell asleep just after they left the state road.

"Here's your turn" Vile announced as he swung the truck to the right after a ride of five miles or so up the valley. "We'll go right on past the farmhouse. It'll be easier to make the hill headin' on up to the lodge if we can get a run at it."

The truck seemed to move through the snow with less trouble once they started up the drive into the Borden property. The Baron wondered why and tried to look out the side window to get the lay of the land, but it was plastered over with snow. He sensed they were going up a long, gradual slope. To no one in particular, Vile gave the answer. "Looks like Buster got himself all plowed out."

Noting the quizzical look on The Baron's face, Vile explained. "Buster. Buster Bascom. He's your caretaker; the guy who runs the farm here. A losin' proposition, if you ask me. No farm in this rocky country ever made more than just enough to keep from goin' to the poorhouse. Of course, half of Buster's problem is the hired help he gets. The last one wasn't worth as much as two dead men. On the other hand, the whole idea of runnin' this farm is to lose money, so I've heard tell. Somethin' about taxes, I guess, but you'd know more about that than I do."

Vile then turned his monologue back to the first subject and left philosophy behind. "Buster's got a tractor, so he keeps himself plowed out. I 'spect he ain't plowed the road on up to the lodge though. No need to. Ain't nobody up there. We'll soon find out."

The Baron had the impression the road was leveling off somewhat. He also realized Vile was pressing down hard on the accelerator and that the truck was gaining speed. "Hang on" Vile warned, "Because here we go."

The truck turned sharply right, the back wheels spun and the chains clanked as they bucked through a bank of snow. The impact jarred the snow loose from the side window and The Baron could see a plowed roadway heading off between two rows of tall trees toward some lights flickering in the distance. At least it seemed like a distance; he couldn't really tell through the dense snowfall.

"That's the farmhouse. Buster'll wonder what damn fool is out on a night like this. But we ain't stoppin' to tell him."

The truck moved steadily onward. The slope steepened and soon The Baron saw the lights of the farmhouse far below. He noticed that the road they were on was a narrow one, terraced into the side of the hill. Now and then, they hit a drift of deeper snow. As the truck fishtailed its way through, The Baron saw they were perilously close to the edge of the drop-off on his side. Vile seemed unconcerned; he hunched over the steering wheel and peered into the curtain of snow trying to make out the track of the unplowed road ahead. Finally, they leveled off and entered a deep woods. The snow was not so deep here. The trees sheltered the road and opened up into an avenue that continued on.

"Clear sailin' now" Vile declared. "We're almost there. The lake's up ahead."

The Baron took his word for it. He couldn't see it. The road swung right, dropped into a dip, and went over a stone bridge, which The Baron assumed crossed the outlet of the lake. A short distance past that, the road made a sweeping turn to the left. Just beyond, Vile turned a sharp left and brought the truck to a halt.

"Here we are" he announced as he climbed out. "Get the key, Spencer."

The Baron climbed down on his side of the truck, with Spencer following. He watched curiously as Spencer waded through the snow to a large maple tree that grew in the middle of what seemed to be a spacious lawn. He brushed the snow away from a gaping knothole about six feet up the tree and reached in. He took something out of the back of the knothole and returned to the truck. The Baron saw he was holding a metal ring about six inches in diameter with a key on it. He handed the key ring to his father, who walked to the back door of the lodge, inserted the key in the lock, turned it, opened the door, and swung it wide. He handed the ring back to Spencer.

"Here" Vile said, "Better put it back before we forget to." Looking then at The Baron, who stood open-mouthed at the whole tableau, he explained. "They always keep that key hidden there in case of an emergency. Guess we're one, wouldn't you say? Don't look so surprised, everybody around here knows about it. You might's well too."

With that, he and Spencer started unloading the suitcases and boxes of supplies. The Baron looked around. The large, three-story lodge loomed in front of him. It was just as his grandfather had described it so many times. it was massive all right and somehow looked out of place here in the deep woods, perched on the edge of an open bluff, which he knew looked off into the valley. The lower story was constructed of huge stones, which made the lodge look bigger than it really was. It was impressive and, he expected, larger than any other residence in this remote valley, or in the whole Catskills, for that matter. The upper two stories were of wood, logs actually, with the bark still on them. That was as much of an inspection of his surroundings as he was able to make. Vile and Spencer had completed the unloading and were ready to leave. The Baron reached for his wallet, took out a twenty-dollar bill, and handed it to Vile. The trip had been worth the extra ten dollars, but Vile would have none of that. He handed a ten-dollar bill back to The Baron.

"I contracted for up to twenty dollars, as you'll remember, no more. I've checked inside; the electricity's on, so's the heat, but it was turned way down, so I turned it up. The water's off though. Buster'll have to turn that on for you. I'd do it, but I ain't got time. I've got to get Spencer on home, his mother will be wonderin' about him. I'll stop at the farmhouse and tell Buster you're here."

Without any further goodbye, Vile DeSilva climbed into the truck—Spencer was already half-asleep on the passenger's side—started the motor, threw it into reverse, spun the wheels as he backed out of the parking area, whipped the steering wheel to the left, and drove rapidly down the drive, spraying a cloud of snow behind.

The Baron watched them leave and waited until the sound of their going and the track of their headlights faded into the dark and the distance. He turned then and entered the hallway beyond the still-open door. The Baron had come home—to the home he had never known.

7.
Thursday, October 22, 1964

EVEN THOUGH it had been a late night—or, maybe, early morning was a better way to put it—Ward Eastman awoke at his usual time. He was a firm believer in the old saying, "Get up early, more people die in bed than anywhere else." Old habits were hard to break. He had been getting up at the same time for over fifty years and wasn't going to change now just because he had added a few hours on the end of the previous day. Besides, he had slept more than an hour in the truck on the way home.

As he went downstairs, he realized it was brighter outside than it should have been that time of the morning. Had he overslept, after all? He glanced at the clock as he went into the kitchen. No, it was the same time—within a minute or two—as it was every morning when he looked at it. He pulled back the curtain to check the thermometer just outside the back window—another morning ritual—and saw the ground was covered by a dusting of snow. It was the white of the snow that added light to the dark of the early morning. Must be the rain turned to snow before it stopped, he thought, noting the thermometer was down to 28 degrees and the sky was clear. Perfect weather for running line in the woods, he reflected, recalling similar days in the past.

A bit later, as he sat at the kitchen table drinking his single cup of coffee, he realized for the first time that the survey of the Borden property might have come abruptly to an end. He didn't have a contract because The Baron wouldn't consider one.

"I'll tell you what I want done, you do it, and you'll get paid," The Baron had told him when he brought up the subject of a contract. "You send me a bill at the end of every month along with a report of what you accomplished and the number of hours you and your men spent on the job and, if I think you earned what you billed, you'll get your money."

It seemed a risky way to undertake a survey the extent of this one, but Ward knew that whatever other faults The Baron had, evading a bill or a debt that was fair and honest wasn't one of them. Every monthly bill sent out so far had been paid by return mail. He supposed it would be some months before the estate was settled. He had read the will of old Orson Borden and had copied it out from the records in the Surrogate's Office down in Kingston as a part of his research before starting the survey. He knew the run of the property, from the oldest son to the oldest son and all that. He was sure The Baron had no children of his own, at least none that he acknowledged. He didn't know Lincoln Borden—or any of the others in the family, except Jen, that is, because The Baron wouldn't allow them on the property. With The Baron gone, Lincoln was now the oldest son and the property would be his.

Ward wasn't sure where Lincoln lived or what his profession was, but he did recall someone saying he owned his grandfather's brownstone in the city. He had heard that Jessie, his mother, had returned to France soon after being notified that Nicholas was "Missing and Presumed Dead" in the Korean War. Beyond that, Ward didn't know anything more about the present generation of the Bordens. He had almost forgotten about Jen though, because, like everyone else who knew her, she didn't seem like a Borden.

She had married Amos Kirk before she turned twenty and the two of them lived on the Kirk family farm in the valley not far up from Milltown. They boarded horses, kept some of their own, and were known far and wide for their equestrian abilities. Talk was they once were going to try out for the Olympic team, but they didn't, being satisfied with winning competitions in dressage, jumping, and three-day events all across the state and, occasionally, farther afield. That fit Jen's style, but what she did otherwise raised a few eyebrows.

She was a farrier; that is, she shoed horses and was as good at it as they come. She and Amos were well-known for their blacksmithing skills and were frequently called by a number of the horsemen in the East. While they could have named their price at any of the big horse farms down in the Bluegrass Country, they preferred their own small place nestled in the craggy Catskills. The only drawback, as far as Jen was concerned, was living that close to The Baron, who she hated with a passion.

Ward realized with a start that he was unconsciously totting up a list of murder suspects. Disgusted with himself (After that other murder, he vowed not to get involved in another one.), he stood up, downed the rest of his coffee, which had gone cold, and went out the back door. Trooper Burgin wanted him to be at the cabin first thing in the morning and he wasn't going to irritate him any further by being late.

By the time he reached Pine Hill, the dusting of snow had increased to two or three inches. It didn't make much difference in the driving because the road crews had been out to clear it away. It always seemed like the road crews couldn't wait for winter. When the first snow came, they were out long before daylight with plows running in every direction even if the snow was only an inch or so deep. So it was this morning. It wasn't really that much, but the plows had come and gone more than once before Ward crested the hill at Highmount. Cynic that he was, Ward supposed it was the overtime pay that brought the road men out of their warm beds and onto the cold highways rather than a sense of duty to the taxpayers.

The snow was about the same depth in the parking lot at the end of the road up Indian Brook. Ward expected to see a number of people because it was obvious more than a few vehicles had been over the unplowed town road ahead of him, but he wasn't prepared for the crowd that was standing about, hands in their pockets, trying to keep warm. He knew then he was late. As he turned the truck around, maneuvering it back and forth in the small space left at the front of the parking lot, Sergeant Burgin moved out of the cluster of men toward him. When he reached the truck, Ward rolled down the window.

"We've been waiting for you," the sergeant said cordially. "Since the road through the woods isn't plowed, we hope you'll agree to use your truck to break trail up to the cabin. You know the twists and turns of the road better than any of the rest of us."

"Sure," Ward assented. "Let me get turned back around. Can you get a way cleared through to the gate?"

That was easier asked than accomplished, but with much confusion and, wonderfully, no dented fenders, Burgin got the drivers to shift a number of the vehicles and the way was opened. Burgin gave instructions to most of the men—some of whom Ward recognized, but more that he didn't—telling them who was to ride with whom, who was to stay put, and probably, who was to make the coffee-and-doughnut run. Well, Ward wasn't sure about that last, but from his past associations with the State police, he knew the morning and afternoon coffee breaks were not to be missed, no matter about bank robberies, murders, and such.

Orders given, Sergeant Burgin climbed into the cab of Ward's truck followed by another man. "This is Lieutenant Morrissy, Bill Morrissy, from the headquarters over in Liberty. His jurisdiction covers Ulster and Sullivan counties and he'll be in charge of the murder investigation."

That, decided Ward, explained Burgin's quiet, but efficient, manner this morning. It was an improvement over his irascibility of the night before. He leaned across Burgin to shake hands with Morrissy, who said how much they all appreciated Ward's help and cooperation.

The one-lane track on up the valley didn't have any deeper snow than covered the ground back in Milltown, but it did hide the humps and bumps. Ward drove slow, traveling in a lower gear; he half-wished Bruce was along to take the road at a faster clip that would jolt his passengers a time or two. He saw a regular train of cars following when he glanced in the rearview mirror.

Noticing that Ward had spotted the entourage, Burgin explained. "Since this whole thing involves two jurisdictions—thanks to you—we've got two of everything coming along. Two sheriffs, two State police units, two local enforcement people. By the way, who did Hardenbergh send?" Burgin asked, turning to Morrissy."

Dave Hoagland, the supervisor. When I called him last night, he said they didn't have a police force over there and he'd have to come himself. He's riding with the Ulster County sheriff."

Burgin turned back to Ward, "We've got a complete investigation team, fingerprint experts, photographers, ballistics people, even dogs and handlers. We thought they might be able to pick up a scent and follow the trail left by the murderer. That looks like a lost cause now, what with this snow covering the ground."

They reached the cabin with no mishaps, which was a surprise. Ward had expected at least one car to get stuck or slip off the road, but all stayed carefully in the tracks Ward's truck made ahead of them. It might be a different story when they left at the end of the day. By then, the sun would have warmed things up, the slight frost that hardened the ground would have thawed, the snow would have melted, and the pure white landscape that now greeted them would have turned to mud. Anticipating the worst, Ward pulled to the side at the entrance to the clearing and waved the other vehicles past. After Burgin and Morrissy got out, he turned the truck around and parked it in the road, heading out, first in line.

Trooper King, the one with no hat, and his partner stepped out of the cabin to greet the arriving official force. They had spent the night at the cabin, watching over it as instructed. When the snow started, Burgin had decided not to send in other troopers to relieve them because of the uncertainty of road conditions and the depth of the snow at the head of the valley, so the two of them had put in all-night duty.

The law enforcement people went about their business with efficiency and dispatch. They knew their jobs; they had been through it all before although probably not in a spot as remote as this. As predicted, the scheme with the dogs didn't work. If they did pick up a scent in the cabin—and their handlers weren't even sure of that—they lost it as soon as they came outside in the snow. Once that experiment had been tried, the rest of the investigators moved across the clearing and into the cabin. Ward stayed back by his truck; he knew he would be out of place in there and, with so many people at work, adding one more to the crowd inside would only contribute to the confusion. If they wanted him, he was sure they'd let him know. Besides, he assured himself once more, he was going to stay as far from this one as he could get. He carefully filled and packed his pipe, lit it on one match as usual, puffed contentedly a few times, moved out into the sun that had now reached into the clearing, and found a comfortable fender to lean against as he waited.

It was almost two hours before Morrissy and Burgin emerged from the cabin. They walked to where Ward Eastman stood, by that time enjoying his second pipe. It was Morrissy who spoke.

"We've got about all out of there we can get and it looks like it would be a waste of time to send trackers out to look for some trail the murderer might have left. I wonder if you'd mind coming into the cabin and telling us how things were when you got here yesterday?"

Ward nodded his agreement, tapped out his pipe on the bumper of the police car he was leaning on, and followed them into the cabin. The interior looked no different than it had the day before; if anything had been moved during the investigation, it had been put back exactly in the same place. The patch of blood in front of the fireplace and the trail of it leading to the back window were still there, although now somewhat faded. It had turned more brown than red as it dried and presented a less gruesome sight. The fact that the body wasn't there made the atmosphere less forbidding. The window shade was still in a heap by the back window, but the one shell casing Burgin had left last evening was gone. Ward assumed it would soon be on its way to the ballistics lab or wherever it was they sent such things.

"I know you went over everything with Sergeant Burgin yesterday, but I'd like to hear the story myself. The officer here will take it all down so we'll have a record," Morrissy said, waving in the direction of a uniformed trooper who sat at the desk facing the big front window, a stenographer's pad open before him. "I'll let you run through it all without stopping," Morrissy continued. "If we have any questions, we'll hold them until you've finished."

Ward took his time relating the events of the day before, trying to recall every detail and not omit anything. Throughout Ward's narrative, Morrissy sat at the dining table occasionally making notations in a small, leather-covered notebook. Burgin sat on the couch in front of the fireplace, listening intently, but clearly now in second position as far as the investigation was concerned. Ward sat at the table across from Morrissy and continued without stopping for well over half an hour. When he paused at the point in his story where Burgin and the others had arrived, Morrissy nodded his head, and flipped back the pages in his notebook.

Finding what he wanted, he looked up and asked, "Can you be specific about the times you and your crew did certain things? We're trying to derive a timetable of Borden's movements yesterday morning. Let me tell you what we have so far.

"The coroners—both of them—have placed the time of death at sometime between ten o'clock in the morning and early afternoon.

They can't get it any closer than that. However, from your observation that the pool of blood by the fireplace—obviously marking where he fell after he was shot—appeared to have dried much more than the blood on the floor where the body lay, it seems he must have been shot earlier than that. In other words, Borden lived for some undetermined length of time after, so that moves up the time of the actual shooting.

"We talked to the couple that takes care of the lodge—the wife does the cooking, laundry, and such and the husband does the cleaning and sees that things run right, acts like kind of a butler or major-domo. They tell us Borden was a creature of habit; that is, he did the same thing at the same time every morning. He got up early—at six o'clock—took a shower, got dressed for the day, had a cup of coffee while he worked at his desk in the den, and then went for a walk. The only thing that varied was where he walked; he changed the route for variety, I guess, and to inspect various parts of the property. When he returned to the lodge from his walk, he had breakfast, always the same thing and always at the same time. The cook was to have it ready to serve the instant he sat down at the dining-room table and she always did, she says, because that was the understanding when they were hired years ago and she had the impression that, if she was late, Borden would fire her and her husband immediately. Sounds like a nice guy, don't you think?"

Ward nodded noncommittally. He wasn't taking sides one way or the other in this one and the question had been rhetorical anyway.

Morrissy continued, "The cook and her husband say that yesterday morning was different. Borden was up at the same time, took his shower, dressed, came down to the kitchen, picked up his cup of coffee from the cook, and carried it into the den. They say he was there only a minute or two. Then he came rushing down the hall, past the kitchen, out the back door, and jumped in his truck. He tore off down the driveway and that's the last they ever saw of him. That was at 7:40AM. They can be sure of that because of the exact time schedule he followed every day."

Now, back to you. When did you and your guys get to the gate at the end of the town road?"

Ward thought a moment or two, trying to remember anything that would tie down the time precisely. "Well, we're not as exact as all that, but getting started yesterday wasn't out of the ordinary, so we must have reached the gate about 8:45AM or so, give or take a few minutes either way."

"And you say you didn't see Borden or anyone else all day and were never out of sight of the road leading up to the cabin?"

"That's right," Ward answered. "At least one of us was in the road every minute of the day."

Looking at Burgin, Morrissy concluded, "Just as we thought. That means Borden probably came directly here once he roared out of the lodge. Something he saw or found in the den must have caused him to change his morning itinerary. We'll go there next."

Turning back to Ward, he continued the questioning. "Did you hear anything during the morning? A distant gunshot? Some noise off in the woods you might have thought was a deer or some other large animal?"

Ward shook his head negatively. "No, but we make quite a little noise ourselves, hollering distances and instructions back and forth. If anyone had been coming out the road, they would have heard us long before we saw or heard them. Especially if they were on the lookout and didn't want anyone to know they were there."

"I understand you made quite a thorough search of the cabin yourself. Did anything in particular attract your attention?"

"Well, yes, two things," Ward answered. "First, both doors and all the windows were locked from the inside. That doesn't really mean much after the fact because the front door has a snap lock that can be set from the inside so it locks when the door is closed. So, the murderer could have left that way. But the question is, how did he—or she—get in? Either The Baron knew who it was and they came in together once he arrived, or The Baron was here first and let him in or whoever it was had a key. If the latter, where did he get a key and where is it now? The only keys I saw were The Baron's and they laid on the desk."

Morrissy nodded, agreeing with that analysis, and indicated that Ward should continue.

"Second is the fire in the fireplace. I see you sifted the ashes that are there. Did you find anything?"

Morrissy shook his head and Ward continued. "A good fire had been burning there early in the day. When we got here in the middle of the afternoon, the ashes were still warm. In fact, a few coals were glowing down at the bottom. Somebody had sure made themselves at home. I'd guess it was the murderer. He must have been the first one here, built a fire to get warm, and just waited for The Baron to show up. He must have known he was coming. How he knew is a question you'll have to answer."

"That's just what we're going to try to do now," Morrissy agreed. "Unless you've got some other thoughts to tell us, we'll get on our way to the lodge. Since we're riding with you, you might as well come along."

The others had been waiting outside in the clearing while the interrogation was going on. (That's what it was, Ward had no doubt, regardless of how friendly Morrissy had been.) They stood in small groups taking in the sun that now warmed the October day. Morrissy detailed each of them to one assignment or another, asking the fingerprint officer and the photographer to follow Ward's truck to the lodge.

Ward climbed in his pickup at the edge of the clearing and waited. He noted the snow was mostly gone, having all melted except for a patch here and there under the shade of some scattered hemlocks. The ground had softened and he knew the tracks in the road would turn to mud as the first couple of vehicles passed.

Instructions all given, Morrissy and Burgin climbed into the cab with Ward. "I want to know how far it is from here to the gate and from the gate to the lodge," Morrissy said. "Set the zero on the trip gauge of your speedometer. If a vehicle didn't pass you yesterday, then whoever it was had to walk. I want to see just how long a hike it is. It might help narrow down our list of suspects."

Ward leaned over and pushed the small button that set the trip mileage back to zero. He knew how far it was, to the foot, for both distances. They had surveyed these and all the other roads and trails on the property so they could be accurately plotted on the final map. It was one and one-half miles to the gate and a little over two miles from there to the lodge, but he didn't say anything knowing that Morrissy would watch the mileage roll up on the gauge anyway. He also decided not to mention the foot trail that ran directly from the lodge to the cabin. It was two and one-half miles long, being the hypotenuse, more or less, of the right triangle created by it and the roads. He'd wait until things quieted down some before bringing that up.

The ride out to the gate was uneventful as far as the pickup and the car in back of it were concerned. It was the third vehicle that got stuck in the mud where the road crossed a small run of water. When

Ward, glancing in his rearview mirror, noticed the widening gap between the first two cars behind the truck, he braked to a stop and told Morrissy it looked like a problem back there. They all climbed down and walked to the stalled car; sure enough, it was stuck, the rear wheels half-buried in the brown muck. That didn't deter the driver, however. He gave it all he had, pressing the accelerator to the floor. The wheels spun, digging a deeper hole and spraying mud over the car behind.

"Shut down the engine," Morrissy hollered and shook his head as he viewed the impasse created by the mired car. "Stay right there, we'll get word to Tom Smythe at the Sunoco station down in Milltown to send up his wrecker. Damn, damn, and damn."

Ward smiled to himself as they resumed their trip out to the gate leaving behind the stuck car and all those in back of it along with their occupants, including the dogs. Bill Irwin was on duty when they arrived. Morrissy told him of the problem on up the road and sent him into town with orders to hire out Tom Smythe to come and make things right. Ward looked at the trip mileage and noted they had come just a little over 1.5 miles from the cabin. He left the indicator at that so they could get the total mileage to the lodge, which read out to be 3.6 miles once they reached there.

Ward had been to the lodge a number of times over the past year or so. They had run the roads to and from it and had tied in the lodge itself on their traverse. They had measured the many sides of it and the sides of all the outbuildings as well. And he had met with The Baron there a few times to discuss various aspects of the survey. These meetings had always taken place in the den and that's where Morrissy asked the butler to take them. Down the long hall they went, past the kitchen and dining areas, through the large sitting room, past the stairs, and on into the den.

The den was a large room with French doors that opened onto the back lawn and looked out to the pond. The walls were lined with bookshelves, all filled with leathery volumes that had sat there for generations. The furniture was massive to match the huge fireplace that jutted out from the back wall. It was The Baron's room, all right, the open wall spaces between the bookshelves were hung with memorabilia recalling his days with the Resistance in France. Only one photograph was displayed; it was a framed snapshot of Frederick, togged out in a fisherman's regalia, that stood on the corner of the desk.

All this was superfluous, however. It was the two wall hangings next to the desk that drew their attention. The first was a large board with a number of hooks arranged in rows up and down and across. These were hung with keys and a label above each hook told what the key was for: "Lodge, Front Door," "Garage, First Bay," "Well House," "Gate, Indian Brook Parking Area," etc. Each hook held two keys; each hook except one, that is. The hook labeled "Hunting Cabin, Front Door" held only one key.

Hanging above the key board was a recessed display box lined with red velvet. A small, lettered, gold plaque affixed to the front of the box stated; "Presented to Barron Borden—For Service Given—by Charles De Gaulle—June, 1945." Set in the velvet lining was a pistol; it was a .45, Ward knew that much. But it was not the single pistol that they noticed. It was the fact that the lining was formed to display two pistols and the second one was not there.

"Don't touch anything," Morrissy cautioned even though he knew the warning hardly needed to be said. "Get the fingerprint and photo guys in here," he directed Burgin. "And tell that butler we want to talk to him. Not in here. In the sitting room."

Turning to Ward, he said, "I don't expect fingerprints will turn up anything. All he got up in the cabin was one set. They were all over everything and must belong to Borden. Whoever did this wasn't lacking for intelligence. Still, we've got to cover every base."

With that Morrissy strode out into the sitting room where they met Burgin returning with the photographer and the fingerprint officer, each loaded down with the impedimenta of their trade. He gave them instructions detailing what he wanted and then motioned to Jacques, the butler, who stood waiting at the hallway entrance to the room.

"Take a seat here on the couch, Jacques," Morrissy invited. "We want to ask you a few questions. First of all, I know your employer was very possessive about his personal property, but I assume you were permitted in the den to clean it. Is that correct?"

Jacques, obviously nervous (Ward wondered if he was nervous about the questioning and the circumstances behind it or if it was because he was sitting somewhere he had never before been allowed to sit.), nodded his head and explained, "Yes, I clean the den every Thursday, right after Mr. Borden's breakfast. I didn't this morning because of what has happened and I wasn't sure just what we should do or shouldn't do."

"I'm glad you didn't," Morrissy approved. "I will have to ask you not to clean anything in there for the next few days. We may need to look the room over again. Now, does the pistol display next to the desk have only one pistol or did it have two?"

"Oh, my, two," Jacques fussed. "They were Mr. Borden's proudest possession. He used them for target shooting on the range back of the garage. He always cleaned them after and took very good care of them."

"About the keys. Did every hook have two keys hanging on it or did some have only one?"

Again Jacques was very positive. "Two keys on each hook. They were the spare keys. Mr. Borden had another full set of keys that hang on large rings in the little coat room near the kitchen door. Each ring is for a certain part of the property—one for the farm, one for the cabin, one for the main lodge, and so on. When he went to one of those places he took that key ring with him and returned it when he came back. He had another key ring he always carried with him—that one had the keys to the truck and the car and the front door here. I can show you where the key rings are hung."

"I wish you would," Morrissy said and they all trooped down the hall toward the back door. Opposite the entrance to the kitchen, a door opened into a small room obviously used as a place to leave coats, boots, and other outdoor clothes. Just inside this door, a number of hooks were arranged on the wall. Each was labeled: "Farm," "Lodge," "Cabin," "Garage," etc. The hook labeled "Cabin" was empty.

Turning to Ward, Morrissy concluded, "That's the ring you found on the desk at the cabin. One of them anyway, the other must be the one with the keys to the truck that's parked up there. Borden must have grabbed the cabin key ring when he bolted out of here yesterday morning. What do you suppose prompted him to go to the cabin anyway?"

Ward shrugged his shoulders. "Who knows. Maybe whoever it was left a note on his desk telling him he'd be at the cabin. It seems obvious that someone was here and took the pistol and one of the keys to the cabin. He very well could have left a note while he was here."

Morrissy agreed. "I think you've got that right." He then asked Jacques, "Is the lodge locked up every night?"

"Oh, yes," Jacques replied. "That's the last thing my wife and I do every night when we leave. We live in an apartment over the garage. It's out of sight from the lodge on up the road there behind the trees and very pleasant for the two of us."

Morrissy continued his questioning. "Have you noticed any signs of a door or a window being forced open? Could someone have broken in?"

Jacques laughed in reply. "Oh, no. No one would have to break in. A key to the back door hangs on a nail in a knothole in that big maple tree out there in the middle of the yard."

Ward nodded in agreement. "Everybody in the valley knows about that key. It's hung there for years, so they tell me. It always seemed somewhat of an anomaly—The Baron was so particular about having everything locked up, but he left that key hanging out there."

"Let's see if it's still there," Morrissy said and headed out the back door. He turned quickly when he reached the tree—the knothole was too high for him to see in it. "Jacques, do you have something I can stand on?"

Jacques did. He went back into the house and came back carrying a five-foot stepladder. Morrissy propped it against the tree, climbed up, and peered into the knothole.

"Yes. There it is," he announced. "We better get it dusted for prints. Whoever did this must have known about the key, used it to get into the lodge, took the pistol and key, and left a note or something that brought Borden to the cabin. Then he locked the door, hung the key up here, and walked back to the cabin. It must have been some walk in the middle of the night."

Well, Ward decided, the time had come to tell Morrissy about the trail. "It's not quite as long a walk as you think. Since whoever it was seemed to know his way around the lodge and the cabin so well, he probably knew about the trail that runs between the two. It's a shorter route. Cuts the distance down some."

Morrissy looked down from the ladder and snapped at Ward, "How come you didn't tell us about that before?"

"Because until we got here, I didn't know your murderer had been here any more than you did," Ward retorted.

"Well, true enough," Morrissy acknowledged as he climbed down from the ladder. "I think we should have a look at that trail before dark puts us off 'til tomorrow."

That startled Ward Eastman. Up until then he hadn't realized how far the day had progressed. It was nearly two o'clock and they hadn't stopped for lunch. It had been a full and busy day that had begun before light and seemed likely to continue on after dark. While the trail was a short cut, it was still a couple of miles long. He wasn't worried about making the hike himself in well less than an hour, but he did wonder just how long it was going to take Morrissy and Burgin, who were not used to that sort of thing. He knew they'd have to go slow and take time to look for traces of someone passing along the trail in the last forty-eight hours. And he was sure the regulation shoes both troopers wore were not made for walking the Catskills' trails.

By that time, the troopers who had been in the den emerged from the lodge. Morrissy explained about the key in the knothole and told them what he wanted in the way of photographs and fingerprints. He then asked Ward if it didn't make sense to have a vehicle driven up to the cabin to wait for them there rather than them hiking back to the lodge. Of course, Ward agreed with that, but hoped they didn't have to go through another stuck-in-the-mud episode.

"I know what you're thinking," Morrissy grinned as if he had read Ward's mind. "I'll make sure we've got a competent driver with the right kind of vehicle this time."

Once Morrissy had instructed the two troopers about having a vehicle sent to the cabin, he turned back to Ward, "Now we're set, show us where this trail starts and let's get on our way."

The trail was more than a foot trail. Frederick had built it for Jen back in the days when she first became interested in horses and riding. And that's what it was, a horse trail, although no horses had been on it for the last fifteen years or so—not since The Baron had banned horses from all the trails on the property and from the property itself. It was a gentle trail with a few ups and downs, but no overall rise in elevation because the lodge and the cabin were at just about the same 2250-foot level. It left the lodge road just across the outlet from the pond and Ward started over the wide lawn in that direction with Morrissy and Burgin following.

The trail was already in shadow, being located on the northerly slopes of Spruce Lake Mountain and Tunis Mountain. The leaves were pretty much gone from the trees, all except the browned, parchment-like leaves of the beeches, which rattled in the slight breeze. The rain, snow, and wind of the night before had taken down the few remaining ones and they lay scattered across the trail, covering it like a multi-colored carpet. If someone had walked the trail, which seemed most likely, any traces of that passage would be covered by the layer of leaves and not be readily seen.

The trail was about five feet wide throughout. It was cut into the uphill slope on the right and built up with laid-up stone cribbing on the left. It had been spread with fine crushed stone to preserve it from the ironshod hooves of Jen's horses. It had stood up well from this use and from the years of non-use that followed. It was still maintained by the caretaker, because The Baron had used it regularly on his morning walks. So Ward and his charges found the trail to be free of blowdown and other debris as they went along. It was a pleasant walk, but they weren't out for the enjoyment of it all.

The trail wound around the main northerly ridge of Spruce Lake Mountain, following the contour as it went. It then dipped into the hollow that had been cut by the waters of Tunis Hollow Brook over eons of time and long before it had been given a name. They walked slowly, scanning the ground carefully, but saw nothing other than leaves, twigs, and stones, all of which belonged there. Tunis Hollow Brook was spanned by a sturdy log bridge as was Stovepipe Brook in the next hollow beyond. They paused at both bridges and brushed away the leaves to clear the surface, hoping to find something helpful, but it was of no avail.

It was nearly four o'clock when they reached the cabin. They had found nothing, but probably they hadn't expected to. Still, the effort had to be made. Two pickup trucks, with drivers, were waiting in the clearing. Ward noticed the look of relief on both Morrissy's and Burgin's faces as the trucks came into view. They had been game throughout the hike, but were clearly glad it was over.

Before Morrissy climbed into the cab of the first truck, he thanked Ward for taking the time to guide them over the trail and continued, "I'd appreciate it if you would come into the Milltown barracks tomorrow morning. Bring along any maps you have that show the trails around the mountains here. We've got to figure out how the murderer got into and out of the valley, although I don't know what good that will do us."

Ward agreed to the meeting and added, "I don't want to stick my nose in where it doesn't belong, but I would make a suggestion. You ought to call in the forest rangers who cover this valley and the ones over the ridges. They make regular patrols along the back roads and stop in at the trailhead parking lots and State lean-tos from time to time. They also periodically walk the trails and the boundary lines of the State-owned lands. They may have seen something or, possibly, even noted down the license numbers of any cars they noticed in the parking lots."

"A good suggestion," Morrissy concurred. "We'll do that. See you tomorrow."

Burgin climbed into the cab with Morrissy and the first truck disappeared slowly down the road, now deeply rutted from the heavy use it had seen that day. Ward looked around the clearing as he walked toward the second pickup. All was quiet. The cabin stood mute and serene, but it had a tale of violence to tell. Ward wondered if the tale had an end.

8.
1946-1958

IN THE WINTER MONTHS following the end of the war in 1945, most of the world looked forward to a return to normalcy with the coming of spring. The Cold War, so-called, hadn't yet started although Soviet Russia had already indicated expansionist notions. It was, however, a time of hope.

The residents in the Indian Brook valley were among those who couldn't wait for the warm months ahead. The families who had sent sons off to the faraway places of war were welcoming them home. All, that is, except for those in the two houses where the small white banner with a gold star in the center hung as a sad reminder in the front window. Whole families that had moved to Connecticut and other distant places to work in factories geared to war production returned home and took up lives they had left behind years before. The first day of spring meant the start of the fishing season was less than two weeks away and the valley people anticipated that more than anything else.

Jessie and the Borden siblings were not quite so optimistic. They knew The Baron or, at least, they thought they did. They didn't really believe things would be as they were when Frederick was alive and presided as lord of the manor—or of the lodge, that is. But they did expect to be welcome at the property and to have license as family to roam the trails, mountains, and back country as they had before. But their expectations remained only that; reality was something different.

Change came quickly to the Borden estate once The Baron got his feet on the ground or, actually, in the snow, because the blizzard he arrived in left behind snow that didn't begin to melt until late in March. Even the January thaw that year lasted only two days and what little did melt then quickly froze again when the winter cold returned with a vengeance.

In less than a month after The Baron asserted his ownership of the vast property, all those employed there were fired. Those who were only summer help were notified their services would not be needed for the coming season. Buster Bascom, the caretaker and farmer, was given two weeks notice to move himself and his family out of the farmhouse. They made the deadline, but just barely. Leaving the only home his children had ever known wasn't easy and was made doubly difficult in the middle of a Catskills' winter when nothing much moved to start with. Buster and his wife had been faithful family retainers, as the saying goes, for over fifteen years, but that mattered not a bit.

New people moved in; no one was quite sure where they came from or how they were found so quickly. The answer to those questions was in a law office in far-off Binghamton. During the war, The Baron had become acquainted with a captain in the O.S.S., who was an attorney in civilian life. He was capable and shrewd, with the ability to get things done quickly and without fuss. He was The Baron's kind of person and, even though the war still raged, was retained to be The Baron's lawyer when he succeeded to the Indian Brook property.

It was Gordon Conklin who hired Jacques and his wife. His charge was to find a couple of French name and background who, between them, could run a lodge—cooking, cleaning, and all—and have them on the job by March 1. They were there. It was Conklin who hired Lenny Dunham from somewhere in Pennsylvania to run the farm. Lenny had to be there by February 15—the day Buster was to leave—to take care of the livestock. He was, although his family—a wife and three sons—didn't arrive until three weeks later.

It was The Baron himself, however, who hired Vile DeSilva as stream-watcher and caretaker of the remote regions of the property. The fishing was over for the valley people. No longer would hunters drive the woods to move the deer out of the cloves and hollows or search for bear dens in the jumble of ledges on the upper slopes of Tunis and Twin mountains. Old habits would die hard and it would take someone with a mean streak to convince people who had had the run of the estate for years that their privileges were over. Vile fit the job description.

All that was out of character for the Borden family; at least, those who had known only Frederick Borden thought so. Those who remembered Orson Borden weren't so quick to agree. In fact, they thought The Baron was a chip off the old block, three generations removed.

It was Gordon Conklin who wrote the letter—return receipt requested—to Jessie informing her not to plan on visiting or bringing her children to the lodge or to any other part of the property that summer or any summer or anytime ever while The Baron was still alive. Well, the letter wasn't really that blunt and The Baron was called Mr. Barron Borden in it, but the message was clear; Conklin was especially adroit in constructing letters and legal documents that left no room for misinterpretation. In that, he was an outcast of the legal profession. Jessie was heartbroken; Linc was mad; Nicky swore; Jack was upset; Jen was disgusted—and swore too—and The Mouse fainted. But the idyllic summers were over. The wording of the letter left no doubt that an appeal would not be acknowledged.

Vile DeSilva had a busy early spring—or late winter, as the case may be. The Catskill Mountains never did have an early spring; spring was always late because winter lasted so long. By the end of it most had cabin fever, wives and husbands weren't speaking, dogs growled at everything that moved and some things that didn't, and the snow hung on in the colder hollows well into June. The old timers said things had improved a lot since they were young. "Why, back then, we had winter. Lasted near year 'round. Of course, it made for good loggin'. The only bad skiddin' we had was on bare ground in August after one winter's snow had just gone and the next hadn't quite yet showed up." So they said anyway, punctuating the end of the pronouncement with a brown stream of tobacco juice that hit the dusty ground perilously close to the listener's feet.

But all that strays from the point, which is that Vile DeSilva had a busy time in the month before fishing season opened in 1946. The previous fall Buster Bascom had taken down the signs that hung at intervals along the Indian Brook road to mark the beginning and end of the fishing beats on the stream. These were small signs, about one foot by three, painted white with the name of the beat in black letters. One side of the sign spelled out the name of the beat ending and the other side told what beat was beginning: "Demis Pool begins - Pipe Pool ends," "Pipe Pool begins - Saw Mill ends," "Saw Mill begins - Upper Dam ends," etc. The signs always looked freshly painted, as well they should, because Buster repainted them every winter. He had completed that job before being told he was leaving. The signs were stacked, ready to be put up, in the workshop out by the barn.

It was there Vile found them. Not quite sure what to do with them—he was sure they weren't to be hung—he asked The Baron. The answer was not unexpected, but even Vile thought it a bit drastic. "Bring them to the lodge," he was told, "They'll make a good fire in the fireplace for a couple of cold mornings anyway." Vile did as instructed and the signs that had welcomed a generation of fishermen went up the big stone chimney in smoke.

Vile's next orders were just as drastic and final. He was to build a substantial fence across the small parking lots located along the road where each of the beat signs were normally hung. And he was to put cables across the footpaths that ran from each of the parking lots down to the stream. Finally, he was to nail up "No Trespassing" signs all along the stream; "Close enough so you can see from one to the next." All this was to be done before opening day of the fishing season; "So if someone didn't get the message before, they will then."

As might be expected, a couple really didn't get the message and Vile caught them just as one was guiding a sixteen-inch brown into his net at the lower end of Demis Pool. They seemed to know better than to decline Vile's invitation to follow him in their car as he drove to Milltown where they stopped in to visit the local justice of the peace. They weren't the only ones Vile apprehended that spring. Some he surprised more than once; they were the local outlaws, who considered the posted signs a challenge and were determined to snare as many of The Baron's trout as possible. They were able to elude Vile at first, but they had forgotten he was a bit of an outlaw himself and knew most of the tricks of the trade, so to speak. The Baron had picked the right man for the job. By the time fishing tailed off in the heat and low water of August, the word was out that it wasn't worth the game to try for the fish up in Indian Brook.

The same scenario played out the big-game hunting season that fall. In preparation for that, Vile headed off into the mountains to post the lines of the Borden property. The boundary along most of the mountain land was common with the State-owned lands of the Catskill Forest Preserve. In some places, this line was easy to follow because it had been surveyed by Ward Eastman and his predecessors with the State survey crew and the local forest ranger walked these lines from time to time and kept the tree blazes fresh with yellow paint. In other cases, the boundary hadn't been surveyed by either the State or the Bordens, and neither Vile nor the ranger had any idea where the line was. Vile nailed up his posters where they could best be seen in these areas and, right or wrong, he intended to see that hunters didn't ignore the ultimatum they gave.

The outcome was the same as with the fishermen in the spring. A few tempted fate and tracked deer onto the Borden land only to be taken by surprise when Vile stepped out from behind a rock, his rifle cradled loosely in the crook of his arm. He never raised the rifle, never pointed it toward anyone, but the fact of it being there was enough to convince the transgressor that it was best to go along down the mountain and into town for a visit with the justice.

When the early snows of winter came and the black bears were seeking out their winter dens, the local bear hunters were sure they could get away with a trophy or two. They were a rugged bunch and thought nothing of spending two or three days at a stretch tracking bear over one ridge after another before finally getting in a position to fire that one shot straight to its mark. But even they were not as circumspect as they thought. Just as they were about to approach the rock ledge where they knew the bear was holed up, Vile appeared at the top of the ledge, rifle cradled by his elbow. Not much was said in those instances. Taking their cue from the tales told by the deer hunters and the fishermen before them, they knew they were on their way to town.

It took only a couple years of this before the local gentry realized the Borden property was off limits. It wasn't fenced in, but it might just as well have been. The line of posters that tracked up the mountains, across the ridges, and down the streams was the same as a fence. And if one didn't believe so, he was welcome to try to step across it. Chances were Vile DeSilva would offer him a ride to visit the justice of the peace down in Milltown.

Everyone resented it, of course. After all, they had been allowed to use the property for years as long as they treated it with respect—and they had. It wasn't right, they reasoned, to have something like that taken abruptly away, without any advance warning at all. None found fault with Vile; he was only doing his job. It was The Baron who was the blackguard. He was the one they cursed down in the bar at the Inn Between of an evening. But it was hard to hate someone they never saw and The Baron rarely came into town. He had shut himself off up the valley, behind that line of posters, and he was content. If they were mad at him, well, that was their business, not his.

While the hunters and the fishermen had lost some territory in which to pursue their whims, they weren't entirely out of business. The State owned thousands of acres all over the Catskills and that land was open for hunting. Similarly, the State had acquired public fishing rights on miles and miles of Catskills' waters and these were available to the fishermen. It was a different story and had a far greater effect on those farmers and homeowners up and down the valley where the Borden ownership consisted of the fishing rights to the stream that crossed their land. At least that's what they thought The Baron owned. As it turned out, they were wrong.

Back in the late 1800s and early 1900s when Orson Borden was amassing his Indian Brook property, land was cheap and exclusivity wasn't as important as it was to become fifty years later. (It wasn't that important to anyone except Orson Borden, that is.) Posted signs weren't the common sights they were later to become. Farmers didn't mind if someone fished the streams that ran through their farm or if hunters walked across their fields to get to the woods and hills beyond as long as they didn't break down any fences and closed the gates behind them. Folks were neighborly then (some still are, of course) and willing to share parts of their ownership if it didn't interfere with the farming operation or their own enjoyment of the property.

Once Orson had acquired all the farms and mountain lands that were for sale in the valley (Some weren't, but it was a seller's market with Orson being the only buyer, so he did acquire a few farms that weren't for sale until he showed up with his open checkbook.), miles of Indian Brook still weren't his, so he tried another tactic. Since it was the stream he really wanted and enough upland along the banks to have control over it, he approached the not-for-sale farmers and offered to buy a strip of land that included their stretch of the stream. Most of these were allowing fishermen to use the stream, so Orson's new offer gave them a chance to make a few dollars without really giving up anything. They sold him the strip of land and he gladly paid

$100. or $200., and even more, if the stretch of stream involved was extensive enough to warrant the higher price. In the upper reaches, where the stream was relatively narrow, Orson acquired a strip one hundred feet in width, fifty feet on each side of the center. On the lower and wider reaches, he purchased a total width of two hundred feet.

Of course, selling a strip of land out of the middle of the best bottom land of a farm wasn't really very smart. But these farmers weren't that dumb and, besides, Orson wasn't trying to deprive them of the opportunity to make a living from their farm. Or, to try to make a living, that is, because hardly anyone could do much more than scrape by on those rocky, thin-soiled, and steep lands. So, most of the deeds conveying the strips of land to Orson contained some reservations.

The least complicated of these provided that "the party of the first part [the farmer] reserves a right of way across the said premises [the strip of land] for the purpose of reaching his lands on the northerly side of said premises." Simple enough, the farmer wanted to get from that part of his farm on the road side of the stream to that part of the farm on the back side of the stream. Hardly anyone, even Orson, could object to that.

Some farmers, especially those where the strip of land widened out to two hundred feet, needed to keep some additional rights before they were satisfied. Not only did they need to cross the strip to get to the other side, they wanted "the right to water stock in said stream [the Indian] and to cultivate the lands so devised [the strip of land] if they choose." Others wanted "the right to till and graze the premises herein conveyed [the strip of land again]." And others wanted to reserve "the right to go upon said premises herein conveyed [still the strip of land] for purposes of constructing any docking necessary to hold said stream [the Indian again] in its bounds." In these cases, Orson wasn't completely happy, but it was the best deal he could get, so he took it, thinking all the while that, in time, he would acquire the whole farm anyway.

The most involved and wordy reservation of all was set out in the deed to the two-hundred-foot-wide strip of land across the Kirk farm down the valley. This negotiation dragged on and on and on. Just when Orson thought he had a deal, old Amos Kirk would come up with something else. The Kirk-farm strip was important to Orson. He had already acquired about one mile of stream both upstream and down from the farm and this was the vital acquisition needed to link the two. The one mile downstream ended just a little above the village of Milltown and that was as far down as Orson intended to go, but he couldn't even get to that one-mile stretch unless he was able to purchase the over one-half mile of stream that crossed the Kirk farm. Finally, they did work it out. It took two lawyers to write the deed, one to assure that Amos kept the rights he wanted and the other to assure that Orson placed enough restraints on Amos's rights so that he did acquire something. In years to come, it would take two more lawyers to interpret what Amos really sold and what Orson really bought. Since it did come up again and since it involved The Baron when it did, it might be a good idea to take another reading of this convoluted reservation.

> The first parties [Amos and his wife], however, for themselves, their heirs, and assigns, reserve and except from the above indenture [the deed language conveying the strip of land], a right of way across the said premises [the strip of land] as a means of access to and from the remaining lands [the rest of the Kirk farm across the Indian] of the said first parties and, also, all the trees and timber now growing and being upon said premises, with the right to cross and re-cross said premises for the purpose of removing said timber and, also, the right of tilling and grazing of the land and, also, the right of access to the stream for the use of the water therein for their cattle and domestic use. But in so exercising such reservations and exceptions they are not in any wise to interfere with or infringe on the second partys [Orson Borden's] and his heirs and assigns sole right of the use and occupation thereof for fishing purposes, or in any wise to interfere with the second partys [still Orson Borden's] enjoyment, privileges or rights incidental thereto to patrol the banks of said stream [the Indian] and control thereof, needful or necessary to his, his heirs and assigns full enjoyment of said fishing privileges and stream rights.

It was these last few words, which appeared at the end of the "excepting and reserving" section of most of the stream deeds running to Orson, that gave rise to the myth that all he had acquired was just that, "fishing privileges and stream rights." Those who believed that interpretation hadn't read (or didn't want to read) the main body of the deed, which clearly intended that fee title to the strip of land and to the stream was conveyed subject, of course, to the various reservations.

In later years, the owners of these farms (usually the next generation or two from the original seller), sold off house lots and summer-camp lots that ran back from the road to the stream and the deeds to these lots usually excepted only "the Borden fishing rights." The farmer knew what had been sold to Orson Borden those many years ago, but the buyer didn't. He came from the big city and, therefore, knew more than the farmer did. And if the buyer didn't get a title search or a survey—which most of them didn't—why should the poor, old, hick of a farmer stir things up. After all, the lot was worth a great deal more if the buyer didn't have to worry about anything more than a fisherman being out in the stream now and then. Since the buyer thought he was getting all the other rights to the stream and the land along its banks, he willingly paid over that higher price. Things went along just dandy during Frederick's benevolent ownership of the Borden land, but these new landowners would soon find out The Baron was not the same kindly neighbor.

Conflicts were inevitable once The Baron realized just what his ownership consisted of up and down Indian Brook. In the first few years after he succeeded to the property he and Vile DeSilva concentrated their efforts on ridding the valley of fishermen who couldn't accept the fact that this fine stream and the fish in it were a private right instead of a public one. In time, Vile's persistence won out and the fishermen stopped coming. Oh sure, some still drove up the valley once in awhile and stopped on the bridges spanning the Indian to gaze down into the shaded depths and marvel at the size of the browns and brookies that lay, hardly moving, in the cool waters.

Once the fishing business got settled down, The Baron spent his time trying to sort out the many deeds, maps, title searches, letters, and legal memoranda that held the answer to what he owned and where it was. He found all these papers crammed into a large, battered portmanteau stuck in the corner of the den behind the desk. It obviously dated back to Orson's time and had been used by him and, later, by Frederick as a place to file the documents having to do with title to the property. File is probably not the correct term, because the papers were in no discernible order and followed no system except the latest documents were on top and the early ones were on the bottom.

He wasn't able to accomplish much more than arrange the papers in chronological order and that didn't really add to his understanding of the ownership. It soon became clear that someday he was going to have to hire a land surveyor to bring reason out of the chaos the documents represented to him. Until then—and he wasn't ready yet to expend the large amount of money that was going to require—Vile would just have to keep posting where he thought the boundary lines were.

However, The Baron was fascinated by the deeds and the other documents. After reading them over and over, he was finally able to separate the deeds that covered the stream from those that conveyed the larger parcels of land. He then tried to put the stream deeds in order, beginning at the westerly end near Milltown and extending upstream, but didn't have any success at that until he ran across two, single-page, hand-drawn sketches consisting of a number of wavy lines running up and down the pages—representing the stream, he thought—with people's names on the right and left sides of the lines. These names matched the names on the stream deeds he had separated from the others. With that Rosetta stone as the key, he put the stream deeds in the upstream sequence he wanted.

On reading these deeds again, he realized the wording of them varied one to another and that, in some sections of the stream, he held more title than in others. All the deeds, however, conveyed the fee title to a strip of land; it was only in the reservations retained by the sellers that they differed. With the knowledge of the general location of the land described by each stream deed, he and Vile walked up one bank of the Indian and down the other, checking on the uses being made of the various parcels by the adjoining upland owner. They found nothing that wasn't in accord with the deed reservations or, at least, in accord with The Baron's interpretation of what the reservations allowed. So his only problem was that his forebears hadn't acquired the full rights to the land and the stream while they were at it.

All that, however, was before the farms in the valley began to be broken up and sold off in small lots to city folk who were looking for a cool, quiet, and rustic place where they and their families could spend the summers. This change in the countryside (some called it progress) was a gradual thing and the valley of the Indian was, thankfully, one of the last to be discovered by the invading horde.

Alton George was one of the first to recognize that his fields along the stream were worth more subdivided into lots than the two cuttings of hay he took off them each summer. Most of the George farm was on the south side of the road and ran up the northerly slopes of Millbrook Ridge, but it did include about ten acres of flatland between the road and Indian Brook and another ten acres or so across the Indian. The land north of the stream was stepped up in ledges and wasn't good for much except now and then Alton, as his father and his grandfather had done before him, cut down a few of the maple and ash trees that grew there and bucked them up into chunks to be split for firewood. So, back in 1893, when Alton's grandfather sold the two-hundred-foot strip along the Indian to Orson, all he "reserved for himself, his heirs, and assigns" was "the right to cross and recross the said premises for the purpose of access to and from first partys land northerly of said premises.

"The land south of the stream did grow a good crop of hay each year and the half-acre Alton plowed and disked off in one corner did produce nice potatoes. But the George farm had a number of hay fields up on the ridge and room for a whole lot of potato grounds. So when that bunch from Queens or the Bronx or Brooklyn or Jersey City or wherever (Alton never was sure where they were from—everyplace that had more than a hundred people living in it was all the same to him.) came along with cash in hand and offered to buy the flat, he was ready to sell. He had been looking at a new tractor anyway and here was the capital he needed to buy it.

The Gagliardis were from Jersey City—not that Alton cared. The six families of them—cousins and brothers-in-law, old and young, uncles and aunts—had been looking for a nice spot out in the country, on a good road, and next to a stream for two or three years. They knew what they wanted; it had to be large enough so each family could have their own place and yet be small enough so one could step out his back door and see all the rest of them if he wanted to, which wasn't very often. It was a fateful day when they made the left turn off Route 28 at Milltown (all three cars, because it took that many to fit them all in) and headed up the valley of the Indian.

They knew their search was over when they drove around Hemlock Turn and saw Alton George's hay field up ahead. They didn't know it was Hemlock Turn because no hemlock tree was there anymore and they didn't know a hemlock from a redwood anyway. Still, the name had a nice ring to it and a hemlock tree really had grown there once. It was a massive thing, three feet and more across on the stump, growing right at the edge of the road on the outside of the sharp turn and leaning in over it. It had survived just fine when horses and wagons were all that passed by. It was when the automobile came along that it suffered. Leaning over as it did, it shaded the road and the ice never melted there in the winter. More than one unwary driver sailed right across the turn and broadside into the old hemlock. Now and then, alcohol helped out and not a few young lads (Alton George himself once, although he said a deer had run in front of him and he was trying not to hit it.) missed the turn and plowed head-on into the tree. It got pretty well battered over time and, finally, it collapsed in a heavy snowstorm one winter and blocked the road for a couple of days. it took six men and a boy, as the saying goes, to saw it up and draw it off. It was still Hemlock Turn after that and probably always would be, but the Gagliardis didn't care what it was called.

They paid Alton more than the ten acres was worth, but they were willing because the stream went with it subject, of course, to "the Borden fishing rights." They closed the deal in the fall of 1955 and spent the next couple of summers putting up their camps and moving in. Well, two families didn't build anything, they just hauled in trailers, second-hand ones at that. The Baron wasn't very happy when he saw the six dwellings (shacks, he called them) going up on the flat. But all the activity was confined to the open field and was closer to the road than the stream, so he didn't have any say-so about what the Gagliardis were doing.

The next summer, however, on one of his rare trips into Milltown, The Baron noticed the brush behind the shacks had been cleared back to the bank of the Indian. Immediately on returning to the lodge, he telephoned Vile (who still lived on his own place up Blackberry Brook in the next valley) and told him to get on the stream back of Hemlock Turn and find out what was going on.

Vile's report was not good news. The Gagliardis had, indeed, cleared most of the brush right up to the stream bank. And they had built two outdoor fireplaces, two horseshoe pits, and a mowed picnic area well within the one-hundred-foot strip The Baron owned on that side of the stream. Worse yet, they had put a stone and board dam across the stream that backed up a half-acre pond, which they were using as a swimming hole. They had a pump in above that and it fed water to three of the camps. But the battle lines were really drawn when the Gagliardis spotted Vile coming down the stream bank and told him in no uncertain terms to get off their land and on his way. Vile did, which was uncharacteristic of him, but then he had never before been confronted by twenty-four, arm-waving, screaming Neapolitans.

The Gagliardis hadn't bothered about a survey when they bought the land or since. Neither had The Baron, but he'd better get one now, Gordon Conklin advised when called, and that's how Ward Eastman first met The Baron. It was a short telephone conversation that evening. The Baron brusquely told Ward he wanted to see him at the lodge at eight o'clock the next morning, not later, and that was the extent of it. Ward wasn't asked if he could come. It was more like he was summoned, but he would find out that was the normal way The Baron dealt with people. Never mind, it worked. Ward stepped out of his pickup truck in the small parking area at the back door of the lodge at exactly 8:00 AM. It wasn't that Ward Eastman had knuckled under to The Baron like so many others did. To the contrary, The Baron's call was because he needed help and Ward had the expertise to provide that help. He had responded as a professional should when called, no matter who the caller is.

The Baron stood at the kitchen door, opened it to let Ward in, and commanded, "Follow me." Down the long hall they went, through the sprawling sitting room, past the stairs, and into the den. A sheaf of papers, tied with red string, lay in the middle of the desk. Picking up the bundle, The Baron handed it to Ward and motioned him into the chair beside the desk. Dispensing with the formalities of introduction and other niceties, The Baron, in short, clipped sentences, told Ward of his problem with the Gagliardis, using a string of colorful metaphors to describe them.

"Somewhere in that packet of deeds is the one where my great-grandfather bought the land along the stream just above Hemlock Turn. You figure out which one it is. Then, get out there and survey my boundary line. You tell me when you're going to be there and I'll have a crew of men follow behind and build a fence as you go. If you have any questions about title or other legal matters, call my lawyer in Binghamton. I've written down his name and telephone number for you."

With that last, The Baron handed a card to Ward. It was obvious the conversation was over. It wasn't really a conversation because Ward didn't get the chance to say anything. Whatever it was, it was over and Ward could sense that. He got up from the chair and made his own way back to his truck. Hemlock Turn was in Delaware County, so he turned left on Route 28 at Milltown and headed for Delhi, the county seat and site of the county clerk's office. It was going to take some deed research to find out just what his survey assignment was and what else he might be up against.

In amongst all the expletives The Baron had used to describe his antagonists, Ward picked up the name Gagliardi. With that being a rather uncommon name in Delaware County, it didn't take Ward long to find the right reference in the indices even without knowing any of their first names. He noted only one deed to a Gagliardi and that ran from Alton George in 1955. Pulling the deed book and finding the page where it was recorded, he read it a couple of times. It was crudely constructed, obviously not written by a surveyor or an attorney who had any knowledge about writing deeds covering land out in the country, but the intention was clear. It conveyed all of the George farm lying between the town road and the center of Indian Brook, except for a fifty-foot strip along the north line so Alton George and his heirs could reach his land on the north side of the stream.

Ward smiled to himself and shook his head when he saw the only exception was "the Borden fishing rights." There was the root of the conflict just as he had expected. Knowing the Gagliardi parcel was a part of the George farm, he was able to figure out which deed conveyed that part of the stream to Orson Borden. He found the original of it in the packet The Baron had given him and then looked up the record copy of it in the deed books. Of course, it covered more than fishing rights. On the Gagliardi side of the stream (and on the other side as well) it was "a strip of land one hundred feet in width as measured from the center of Indian Brook as it now flows and may hereafter flow." The only exception was for a right of way across the two hundred feet; nothing was said about fireplaces, dams, horseshoe pits, water pumps, lawns, cutting brush, or anything else. The survey problem was clear, but Ward wondered if he would survive the field work of it.

It was a hot day that Saturday. Independence Day had been on Friday, and Ward Eastman picked that weekend for the fence-building survey because it was more probable than not that all the Gagliardis would be there then, more than at any other time. Not that Ward relished the confrontation he knew was coming, but he'd rather tell them just once what the survey was all about and why the boundary line was where it was.

The meeting place and time was Hemlock Turn at 8:30 AM. When Ward arrived with Paul and Phil, his crew in those days, Lenny

Dunham and three of his farm workers were already there. Their truck was loaded down with cedar fence posts, all cut to length and pointed; rolls of 4-foot woven-wire fencing; sledge hammers; post-hole diggers; and anything else that could possibly be needed to build a substantial and permanent fence. They had to wait about ten minutes before Gordon Conklin showed up—Ward had called him a few days before and Gordon agreed he should be there. Right behind Gordon was a State police car with Trooper Burgin at the wheel. While most knew Burgin, Gordon introduced him around and explained that he thought it might be a good idea to have some law enforcement on the scene just in case things got a bit sticky.

Paul and Phil were sent down to the stream with the task of determining the center of it and, then, laying out 100-foot offsets from that line. Lenny and his men unloaded their materials and tools from the truck and carried them down to the stream bank; they would have to wait until the line was actually run before they could start their part of the work for the day. Ward and Gordon walked up the now-mowed stream bank toward the picnic area, where two men were sitting, having their morning coffee and enjoying a cigarette. Burgin stayed in the background, alert to what was going on at all locations and ready to intervene if it became necessary.

Ward and Gordon were only about halfway to the picnic area when one of the men arose and came toward them. "Whether you know it or not, you're on private land and you'd better get off and back where you came from."

It wasn't going to be easy, Ward knew as he continued walking. "We do need to talk to you or whoever is spokesman for your family about whose land this is. If you have a local attorney, you might want to call him."

"It's none of your business whether we have a lawyer or not. But it is my business that you're on our land and you have no right to be here. Now, get off."

That was Burgin's cue and he moved out of the woods where he and Lenny's work force had been waiting. At the same time, and almost simultaneously, the doors of the six camps opened and the Gagliardis, as if summoned by the loud voice of their bellwether, emerged and converged toward Ward and Gordon. Burgin quickened his pace. It wasn't until he spoke that any of the Gagliardis realized he was there.

"Now, whoa back there," Burgin ordered. "These men have something important to tell you. Give them the opportunity to say it. If you have a lawyer in town, call him. We can wait."

They did have a lawyer in town and it took only about twenty minutes for him to get there. Gleason Vredenburgh hadn't been their attorney when they acquired the property—some cousin back in Jersey City had handled that—but he had represented one of the teen-aged sons during some nasty business about a fight with broken beer bottles in the bar at Kelly's Hotel. Until Gleason arrived, it was a standoff. The Gagliardis stood in one group; Ward and Gordon stood together; Burgin strategically placed himself in between. Lenny, still back in the woods downstream, sat on the roll of fence wire and lit up his pipe. The only ones who kept moving were Paul and Phil, working their way upstream, measuring from one side to the other, and driving stakes in the center.

It took about two hours to get things settled. Ward and Gordon were well-armed with deed copies and sketch maps. They were helped by the fact that Gleason Vredenburgh had been entangled before in a couple of disputes where the Borden "fishing rights" were involved. He knew Ward and Gordon held the strong hand, but it took time to convince the Gagliardis. They never were really persuaded, but under Burgin's watchful eye, they did move the picnic tables, the water pump, and their other personal items over the line of stakes Paul and Phil drove in on the 100-foot offset. Lenny and his men waded into the stream and dismantled the dam.

Things went along quickly after that. It was a simple matter to run the traverse along the line once it had been set by measurement from the center of the stream. And Lenny's men were good fence builders; they weren't more than a hundred feet or so behind the transitman all afternoon. By late in the day, the survey was completed, the fence stretched taut from post to post all the way across the field, and the waters of the Indian flowed unimpeded, heading for the East Branch of the Delaware down near Milltown.

The Gagliardis would never forget that day. They swore The Baron would soon hear from their cousin, the lawyer, and all the rest of them, including Burgin, could expect to be sued. None were and The Baron didn't hear from the cousin. The Gagliardis spent the rest of the summer moving their things, including the two trailers, out of the valley. They didn't come back the next summer, but one of the camps mysteriously burned down that fall. They never did return to the valley of the Indian. The field grew up to weeds and brush; the three remaining camp buildings, they were kind of ramshackle anyway, collapsed under heavy snow in the winter of 1962-63. The wire fence still stood, tight and true, but finally disappeared under a thick growth of blackberry bushes, grape vines, and poison ivy.

In time, the Gagliardis were forgotten by the valley folks. But Burgin remembered them and the threats they had made that Saturday. Ward Eastman remembered them too. One in particular stuck in his mind. While they had been waiting for Gleason Vredenburgh to arrive, a stiff breeze had come up. It was welcome on that hot day. Ward wondered why one of the Gagliardis, a young man in his mid-twenties who kept in the back of the family group, was wearing a suit jacket as hot as it was. The breeze lifted one side of the jacket and Ward glimpsed a handgun stuck in the belt of the man's trousers. No one else had seen it; all were then watching Paul and Phil as they splashed up the center of the stream. But Ward had seen it and he hadn't forgotten.

9.
Friday, October 23, 1964;
Thursday, December 3, 1964

WARD EASTMAN took his time on Friday morning. Morrissy hadn't specified what time he expected him at the barracks in Milltown; in fact, he hadn't said early morning or late morning—just plain morning—and Ward took that to mean the choice was up to him. It wasn't as if he didn't have things to do other than respond to the beck and call of a bunch of public servants. But, they had a job to do just like everyone else and no need making that any tougher than it already was. The first order of the day was to get Bruce and Steve started on their way to begin the survey of the Bush farm over in Lexington. Then he rummaged around the two-car garage he had converted into an office and pulled out every map he could find that delineated the trails and old roads near the Indian Brook valley. Piling these into the seat of the pickup truck, he headed for Milltown. He decided it was a good thing he was drawing retirement because the pay for this police work wouldn't keep a chicken in corn.

It was Burgin who met him when he entered the front door of the barracks. "Say," he greeted Ward, "Do you remember the family that owned the land where we built the fence a few years back?"

"Never'll forget them," Ward replied. "Garibaldis or Cagliostros or Gagliardis or some such they were called. They haven't been around since then that I know of."

"Well, two of them were here earlier this week. Young Al George called in to tell about it. He saw smoke coming up from one of those old derelict cabins three or four days back and thought maybe it was on fire. When he went over to see, he found two young guys with a tent, sleeping bags, packs, all that stuff, cooking their breakfast over a stone fireplace they had put up. He asked who they were and they told him their family owned the land and they were just camping and hiking some of the trails around. He didn't think anymore about it then. They seemed friendly enough, he said."

"I haven't noticed any activity around there in years," Ward offered. "Of course, if they had their camp behind one of those buildings, you couldn't see it anyway, what with all the brush that's grown up on the flat.""That's what I thought," Burgin agreed. "Al says they're gone now. Left a couple of days ago. I'm on my way there now with some men to look around. When you get done with Morrissy, come on up. Maybe you can see something we can't."

Ward took that as kind of a compliment. He said he would come even though he was uneasy about getting any more involved in the investigation. Burgin introduced Ward to the trooper on duty at the desk, telling him Ward was there at Lieutenant Morrissy's request, and departed out the door.

Morrissy wasn't alone in his office. Ward found him talking to Ed Richards, who was in charge of the forest ranger unit of the Conservation Department out of Albany. Ed was an old hand and had been at the Albany post back in the days before Ward retired.

"Since you two know each other, no need for me to explain why you're both here," Morrissy said. "Richards has agreed to call his local rangers together to see if any of them saw or heard anything that might have a bearing on our murder problem. I thought maybe you, Eastman, could explain your thoughts about how the murderer came into and went out of the valley. Then, he'll know which rangers are most likely to be of help."

Ward nodded and Morrissy continued, "Spread your maps out on that table over there under the window where the light's better. I've got some telephone calls to make, but I'll go out front to do that, so I don't bother you."Ward knew the trails and bushwhacks around the Catskills about as well as anyone and had already concluded where the murderer had come from and gone back to. Richards had an Adirondack background and wasn't overly familiar with the Catskills, so Ward laid out his U.S.G.S. sheets and trail maps.

Using his pencil as a pointer, he ran through his theory with Richards. "Here's the cabin where Borden was murdered," he explained, pointing to the small black square on the U.S.G.S. sheet that denoted the building. "A fairly decent road runs to it from the end of the town road, but it's private and gated. It was a public trail once, but the present owner—or the past owner, I guess, because he's the murder victim—closed it off about fifteen or eighteen years ago. The old trail continued on up the thread of the stream and into the saddle between Twin and Indian mountains to where the state land begins. The trail is still distinct enough to be followed without much trouble. It joins the main state trail that runs over the summits of those mountains and beyond. Another state trail drops down Breadloaf Brook on the other side of the ridge and ends at a small parking lot just off the county road along the West Branch of the Neversink. That's where he went, betcha a dollar. See if any of your rangers noticed any cars in that parking lot on Tuesday night/Wednesday morning. At least one was there, I'm sure of it."

Ed Richards concurred. "That's sure the shortest route. It wouldn't make much sense to take either of the longer trails over Twin or Indian or Hawk. This route you've laid out is only about four miles long; one and a half up out of the valley and two and a half down the other side. And the best part from the murderer's standpoint, that is—he'd be in a whole different valley. While everybody's looking for him in the Indian, he's over on the West Branch."

Morrissy returned about then and Ward went over what he and Richards had discussed. "I can't find any fault with your reasoning. See what your rangers can come up with, Richards, and give me a report tomorrow if you can." He reminded Ward that Burgin was expecting him up at Hemlock Turn. "He thinks he's onto something, but I have my doubts."

Ward had his doubts, too. He had made up his mind they were looking for someone who knew his way around the valley; someone who knew about the trail that ran from the lodge to the cabin; someone who knew something that could draw The Baron out of the lodge at a moment's notice and send him on a mad dash up to the cabin. He doubted the Galileos or Garibaldis or whatever their names were fit that picture. But no sense theorizing about that; he was on the fringe of this one and he wasn't going to get any more tangled up in it that he already was, which was too much now when he considered the time he's lost out of his regular schedule.

He walked Ed Richards out to his state car and the two of them stood there a few minutes reminiscing about times past and old friends and coworkers, who were now past too. Ward asked Ed to let him know what the rangers had to report or, perhaps, found. "Just curious, I'm not really involved in this," Ward assured Richards. Ed shook his head knowingly.

As Ward drove out of town, he passed the firehouse and noticed the forest ranger trucks parked there just about filled the open space out front. He saw Frank Borden (no relation to the Indian Brook Bordens) and Byron Hill and some other older rangers he knew in the group waiting for Ed. Frank's district took in most of the area on the Indian Brook side of the range and By's ran up and down the West Branch. They were good rangers, Ward reflected, waving as he drove past; they were conscientious about patrolling the territory assigned to them. If anyone had seen anything—and remembered the details— they would be the ones.

Burgin's patrol car was parked at Hemlock Turn and Ward pulled his truck in behind it. He scrambled down the bank to the stream and walked along it toward the clearing—or what had once been a clearing. He noticed the trees they had blazed to mark the boundary line and smiled at Lenny's fence still stretched tightly from tree to tree. The blazes, now six years old, were beginning to grow over. The fence ran on out of the woods into the brushy area that had once been the lawn mowed by the Gagliardis. (That was their name, he knew it would come to him if he thought about it long enough.) The fence posts and the fence ran straight and true, even covered over with vines and brush.

Burgin heard him coming and waited for him alongside the fence where it passed in back of one of the cabins. He waved Ward to the spot. "This is where their camp was. They cut a hole in the fence, most likely so they could get water out of the brook. You can get through here."

The brush had been cleared away in back of the collapsed cabin and a few field stones had been laid up into a fireplace. The coarse hay and weeds around the fireplace were flattened and Ward could make out the outlines of a tent.

"We've combed over the area quite thoroughly," Burgin advised. "But you take a look around and tell me what you think."

"This is the first anyone has been here in awhile," Ward judged. "You can see the brush they cut down—with a machete, it looks like; and a dull one, at that—is the same age as the rest of it growing all over the old field. The clearing was done only a few days ago."

He walked over to the fireplace and examined it inside and out. "The fireplace is new, too," Ward asserted. "The different shading of some of the stones—even those on the base of the fireplace—indicates they were only recently pried out of the ground. Looks like they were here only a few days—the stones on the inside of the fireplace aren't completely black from the fire. It's a wonder they didn't set the field on fire; they didn't dig down below the duff here in front."

"How many do you think were here?" Burgin asked.

"I'd say two," Ward answered. "The flattened area there and the holes where they set their tent stakes indicated it was a small, two-man tent. By the looks of the matted grass, they had only two sleeping bags."

"That tallies with what Al George says. When he saw the smoke and came down, two of them were here by the fire. After he talked with them a few minutes, he went on into town. He saw a car—took it to be theirs—pulled down into that old log road just past the turn. He said it might have been there before, but since he wasn't looking for one, he could have missed it. He didn't get the license number and isn't even sure what make it was. That was the day you found the body. But it was before Al knew anything about it, so he had no reason to be suspicious about them or the car."

Ward asked the question that was on his mind. "Do you really think those two had something to do with the murder?"

"Well, they had a motive. Remember that day how mad the whole family was and the threats they made? They were going to get all of us, especially Borden. He was the one they blamed for taking away the place they had searched for and worked on for so long. I think it bothered them more and more over the years and a couple of them finally decided to do something about it."

"I won't deny they had the motive; at least, to them it probably seemed like a motive," Ward agreed. "But how did they know about the trail? How did they get Borden to go to the cabin? Why go to the cabin anyway? If they were going to do away with him, why not do it in the lodge?"

"Oh, I'll admit we've got a lot of loose ends, but it's something to start with. We don't have much else at this point."

That much was true, Ward thought. He was glad the puzzle wasn't his. It wasn't like a surveying problem. Then, you at least had a deed to begin with; something you could pick up by the four corners and turn one way and another until it made some kind of sense. Maybe Burgin thought he had one corner of this one, but Ward wasn't so sure.

On the walk back up to Hemlock Turn, Burgin told him most of the family was due to arrive that day. Some were going to stay with the sister at the Kirk place and the rest were booked in the motel/cabins out on Route 28. They weren't yet allowed in the lodge and wouldn't be for a few more days. The investigation there was still going on, so it was off limits until that was over. He'd also heard that the lawyer, Conklin, was in town. He had been at a fishing camp over on the Neversink for the last week or so, but came as soon as word reached him.

"The funeral's tomorrow," Burgin continued. "We released the body. The coroners couldn't tell us much more than we'd already figured out. He died from the two gunshot wounds about midday. He was actually shot some time before, but lived on after. That coincides with the story the butler and his wife gave us about Borden leaving the lodge a little before eight o'clock and with your statement about the time you got there, the still-warm coals you found in the fireplace, and everything else.

"Funeral's private, by the way; if you were thinking about going," Burgin informed him as they reached his car. "Family wanted it that way. Can't imagine many others would go even if they had the chance, unless it was to make darned sure he got put in the ground."

It was the middle of the afternoon by then. Ward realized he'd missed his lunch again and decided that surveying had a lot more regular hours than this police business. Even though it was late in the day, he drove on over to Lexington to see how Bruce and Steve were making out. He'd told them to brush out and set transit stations up the west line of the Bush farm because it was the only line he was sure of. It started on the south bank of the Schoharie and ran up along a stone wall for about twenty chains. It continued on up the ridge for another mile or so, cornering at a pile of stones near the top of Packsaddle Mountain. Ward had been to that corner years before when he was surveying the state land on the West Kill side of the mountain. They'd have to push a compass line from the end of the stone wall up to the pile of stones. He wanted to know how far along they were and if they had found any evidence—old blazes, remains of wire fence or, better yet, old rail fence—along the line on past the end of the stone wall.

While he was anxious to get back to surveying and was really looking forward to the Bush farm survey (He liked the high-mountain, remote surveys, and the five-hundred-acre Bush property was one of those.), he found he couldn't keep his mind on it as he drove along. Instead, he was back in the cabin trying to picture things as they were when he had entered it on Wednesday. Maybe he had seen something important and had forgotten it. Stubbornly, he forced himself to think about the survey, but moments later, he realized he was back along the Indian.

The next morning Ed Richards stopped at Ward's office in Woodland Valley. He didn't really have much to tell him. None of the rangers had noticed anything out of the ordinary. By Hill had seen two cars in the lot at the end of the Breadloaf Brook trail on Wednesday morning, but that wasn't unusual and he hadn't paid them any particular attention. The rangers had walked all the trails in the two valleys, but that didn't turn up anything except the usual candy and chewing gum wrappers. They had come across a few hikers and talked to them, but they weren't of any help either. Ed was on his way back to Albany. He had made his report to Morrissy and, while he was grateful for the rangers' cooperation, he conceded they couldn't be of much further assistance in the investigation. Ed had agreed to keep them and himself on call should Morrissy need them again.

Later that afternoon, Gordon Conklin called and then drove over to Ward's office. He had been to the funeral, the only one there who wasn't immediate family, but The Baron's will appointed him executor of the estate, so he did kind of qualify as quasi-family. Ward hadn't seen Gordon since the day of the Cagliostro (or Garibaldi or whichever) family survey, but they had talked on the telephone quite regularly over the past year or so. Once The Baron had decided to have the entire property surveyed — finally following Gordon's advice—Ward occasionally needed some information from Gordon's files and Gordon kept interested in the progress of the survey.

It was about the survey that Gordon had come. Under the terms of old Orson's will, Lincoln, or Linc as most called him, was now the owner of the Catskills' property. Barron Borden had left no issue (Gordon's term), at least none he ever claimed or knew about, so Linc was now the oldest son of the oldest son and so on. Linc had come for the funeral. Well, they all had—arrived early, Gordon said and he had never before seen such a happy bunch at a funeral.

"Darnedest thing you ever saw," Gordon related. "The local parson read a couple of verses from the Bible and they all stood up and said 'Amen' and that was it. Then, this white-jacketed waiter came in pushing a serving cart. He handed a stemmed glass to each of us and whisked off a white cloth that covered a big ice bucket in the middle of the cart that held two magnums of champagne. The guy popped the corks, poured half a glass for Linc; he sipped it and nodded to the waiter, who then went around and filled all the glasses. Linc motioned us to stand around the closed casket and raised his glass. I thought he was going to deliver a eulogy or something. He just said 'Godspeed.' Everyone else said 'Amen,' I so I did, too. Then, they all drained their glasses, handed them back to the waiter, and walked out. Darnedest thing you ever saw."

"I'm not really surprised. As you and I well know, none of them had any charitable feelings left for The Baron after the way he threw them off the property. Especially Jen, you must remember what he did to her and Amos Kirk."

"Oh yes, I'll never forget that episode," Gordon replied. "Still, the funeral—or celebration may be a better term—was a bit bizarre. You know what ran through my mind after it was over?"

Of course Ward didn't, so he responded with the obligatory question, "No. What?"

"I thought maybe they had gotten together and hired someone to shoot Barron. A hit man or whatever it is they call those kind of people."

"Hit man is as good as anything, I guess," Ward acknowledged. "But your idea is quite far-fetched, I'd say."

"Maybe, but it isn't any more far-fetched than the funeral was. However, that is not why I came to see you. Lincoln Borden and I had a long talk yesterday afternoon. He knew all about the terms of the old will and that once Barron died—was out of the way was how he phrased it—he was the owner of the Catskills' estate. Since he and none of the others had been allowed on the property for so long, he wondered what had been done with it or to it. I brought him up to date about what I knew. Among other things, I told him Barron had retained you to survey all the boundary lines of the property and that you were quite far along. He wants you to finish the job and prepare an overall map. He's got some idea about leasing or renting parts of the property to his brother and sisters. I'm supposed to look over the will and advise him just what he can do or can't do under its terms. Once I do that and you get the map done, he wants to divide the property so that each has some personal control over their share of it. They seem to have talked this over in some detail; it's almost as if they have been planning on it."

"Are they in a real hurry to get the map? We I've got some distance of line yet to run up on Hawk and Twin mountains. Most of the lowland lines are done and the stream is all finished. That was The Baron's top priority."

"No real hurry," Gordon answered. "They're planning on sitting down with the map some time next summer and then decide how they want to divide the property; if they can, which I'm not sure of at this point. The terms of the will are quite restrictive."

"We'll have it by then. We can finish up over the next couple of months. Even if we get deep snow, we can do those back lines on snowshoes; we won't find much evidence along them except for some old blazes and the corners will be witnessed, so we won't need bare ground to find them. I've been to most of them in years gone by anyway."

It was pleasant visiting with Gordon Conklin. If only Ward could have worked through him instead of having to deal directly with The Baron on the survey, it would have saved him a lot of grief. He didn't know Lincoln Borden; he had been banished from the mountains long before Ward had become involved with The Baron and the property. The fact that he had delegated the legal and survey matters to Gordon was a good sign. The remaining time to be spent on the survey should be a lot less contentious than what his experience had been so far, Ward hoped to himself. He almost wished he had a glass of that champagne so he could raise an "Amen," too.

Over the next few weeks, Ward spent most of his time with Bruce and Steve running the lines of the Bush farm. The air was growing colder day by day; the sun was not as warm, and the sky was not as blue either, or so it seemed. On cloudy days, the grayness overhead appeared ominous. The sun came out hardly at all the first week in November. Snow—and a lot of it—was not far off.

They enjoyed working in the chilly, fall weather—all except the transitman, that is. While the others on the crew were chopping line or measuring shots and being warmed by the body heat they generated in the process, the transitman moved only from one side of the transit station to the other, sighting on the backsight and then on the foresight, turning the angle. But even that was better than keeping the survey notes. It was possible to spin angles and read bearings with gloves on, but recording data in the notebook was a barehanded job. On bitter cold days, the sensitivity in frosted fingers was nil, the pencil was difficult to hold, and the resulting scrawl was sometimes hard to figure out. Most times, only the transitman could make sense of the numbers and words and sketches he recorded on those shivery days.

They finished the field work of the Bush farm survey the second week in November. Ward decided to hold off on the computations and mapping until midwinter and spend the remaining good days back in the valley of the Indian. Not many good days were left, however, and by the first of December they were forced inside by an early and prolonged snowstorm. It wasn't a blizzard because it didn't happen all at once, but after a week of it, the ground was blanketed by eighteen inches of snow.

On one of those snowy days, when the three of them were in Kingston to research deeds in the county clerk's office, Ward ran into Bill Morrissy in the courthouse. He was waiting to be called to testify in a case that was being tried in one of the courtrooms on the second floor and was talking with some fellow officers in the lobby. Ward was on his way to search through the old assessment rolls that were stored in the "dungeon" in the basement. They noticed each other at the same time and moved forward to shake hands in greeting.

"I never did thank you for all the time you spent and the help you gave us on the Borden murder," Morrissy said. "I should have acknowledged it by letter and I'm sorry I didn't take the time to write one."

"Don't fret about it," Ward responded. "I just happened to be the one who was there. It could have been anyone. Do you know, that whole business has kind of faded out of my mind. We've been knee-deep in both survey work and snow since then and I haven't really thought about much else. I didn't hear that you arrested anyone. How is the investigation going? Do you have some idea of who did it?"

"Oh, we've had all sorts of ideas, but every one ran into a blank wall. You knew Burgin's theory that someone in the family that owns the land up on the sharp turn did it."

Ward nodded in reply. "I didn't want to discourage him, but I thought that wasn't going anywhere."

"Well, you were right. We did locate the two who were camping on the property and arranged to question them at the state police barracks near their home in New Jersey. They gave us quite a detailed account of where they went and what they did the three or four days they were there. Turns out their car broke down the afternoon before the murder and were at Tom Smythe's garage in Milltown for the rest of the day waiting for the car to be fixed. It wasn't ready by the time the garage closed, so they had supper and spent the night at Kelly's Hotel. When the car was ready about nine or nine-thirty the next morning—which was just about the time Borden was shot—they picked it up, drove back to their camp, and were cooking breakfast when Alton George spotted them. We checked all that out at the garage, the hotel, and with Al and everything fit just the way they said. Burgin was pretty disappointed, but he got over it."

"Seemed to me if they were that mad—and they were at the time we built the fence—they would have done something then, not years later."

Morrissy cautioned, "Not necessarily, some people hold a grudge for years; it churns around inside until finally it gets to be too much to hold in any longer and they erupt. We have kind of a process we go through in our murder investigations. It starts with three questions: Who were the victim's enemies? Who gained by the victim's death? Who had the opportunity to commit the murder?

"As you might imagine, we had quite long lists in answer to the first two questions and a lot of names were on both lists," Morrissy continued. "You know about the other people like the Gagliardis who own property up and down the stream. Once Borden stopped their use of the stream—something they thought they had bought and paid for—they became enemies. And, if he wasn't around any longer, the new owner might let them use the stream again. So, they possibly stood to gain. The same thinking holds for all those who used to hunt or hike on the Borden land."

"Same as the family at Hemlock Turn," Ward interjected. "That would be a long time to hold a grudge."

"We came to the same conclusion," Morrissy agreed, "and put them down at the bottom of the lists. Then we considered those Borden fired back when he first came to the valley. The caretaker, for instance. Bascom, I think his name was, and all the others. They certainly were enemies, but chances are they wouldn't get their jobs back or, wouldn't even want them back, if Borden was gone. We put them down at the bottom of the lists, too."

"Sounds to me like your lists were bottom heavy," Ward chuckled.

"Well, almost," Morrissy allowed. "But we had a few up at the top. The family mostly. Of course, you know about the upset with the oldest sister—half-sister, I mean—and her husband. They own that horse farm just down from Hemlock Turn."

"Oh, yes," Ward said, "I know all about that one. I wasn't directly involved because that question hinged more on law than survey, but I sure know what happened there."

"They certainly were enemies and would really have gained if Borden was no longer around. The same with the rest of the family. They all hated Borden once he threw them off the property. And they would get it back if he was gone. In fact, the oldest half-brother really stood to gain; he would be the one who would end up owning the property. Of course, having to pay the taxes and upkeep on an estate that size isn't much of a gain. Interesting thing about the youngest sister. We learned her husband is a pistol champion and had been a member of the French national team when he was an officer in the French army."

"I didn't know that," Ward replied. "I haven't met them all yet. I have spoken with Lincoln, the oldest, a few times about our survey and I knew the oldest sister before this happened."

"Must be you knew Borden fired DeSilva just a week or so before the murder? Caught him poaching deer. Turns out he had been doing that for years. Catching fish, too, when he wasn't supposed to."

"Vile always had the reputation of a scoundrel," Ward replied. "He was the first one I thought of when I realized The Baron had been shot."

"So much for lists," Morrissy went on. "They fell apart when we got to the third question. Those at the top of both lists—the family members and DeSilva, too—didn't have the opportunity. They were all someplace else, and could prove it, for the time the shooting took place. The oldest sister and her husband were way off in Syracuse at a horse show. The rest were just as far away or further."

Ward didn't get to hear what the other alibis were. Just then a call came down from the second floor of the courthouse that Lieutenant Morrissy was wanted in the courtroom. Morrissy went upstairs and Ward went down. He let himself into the room where the old assessment rolls were kept; he had picked up the key from the treasurer's office back in the county building. The small room was lined with sagging shelves on which the dusty books were stacked. These were separated by town, but weren't in chronological order. The book you really needed was always on the bottom. The only light was a single bulb hanging at the end of a taped-up wire in the center of the room. The only other furnishings were a wooden table and two chairs, all of which wobbled on the uneven floor. One had to be careful moving about; the ceiling was crossed by pipes of the building's hot-water-heating system and most of them were so low that a person passing underneath had to duck to get from one side of the room to the other. All who came to research the assessment rolls called the place "the dungeon" and the name was apt.

Ward noticed none of these things. Instead, he sat silently at the shaky table, the file folder he had brought opened before him. He looked straight ahead, his forehead wrinkled in thought. He had almost forgotten about the murder; his chance meeting with Morrissy had brought it all back. Now he was trying to assimilate what Morrissy had told him with the facts he remembered from the day of the murder and the days following. He shook his head and banged the table with his clinched fist. It wobbled again.

He spoke aloud to himself, while actually addressing the absent Morrissy, "It's all right to go by the book and ask your standard questions, but you should have asked some other ones, too. 'Why did The Baron go to the cabin? And who knew he would go that morning and just at that time?' "

10.
1958-1964

THE FRACAS involving Jen and Amos and the old Kirk place happened not long after the Gagliardis and the fence-building incident.

The Kirk farm was one property removed downstream from the Gagliardis and the Alton George place. Like the George farm, the Kirk lands ranged on both sides of the road and crossed Indian Brook. The house, barn, and other outbuildings were on the wide flat between the stream and the road. The hay fields and plowed grounds were on the south side of the road, stretching terrace-like up the slopes of Millbrook Ridge. All of this land was well-watered by cold-flowing springs and mountain creeks (or cricks in the local vernacular) that kept running even in the driest summers. The land north of the stream was rocky, but covered with scattered groves of trees and open grassy areas. It wasn't much good for growing hay or corn or any garden produce, but it was ideal pasture. However, it was dry; the land was located on the nose of a wide ridge with the streams on each side of it being on the properties adjoining on the east and west. It was barren of springs and the only water available for the stock was Indian Brook itself.

When old Amos Kirk worked the farm and on through the next generation, it was a dairy farm and a good one. It ran an all-Holstein herd and shipped more milk out to the creamery in Milltown than any other farm for miles around. The cows and young stock pastured on the north side of the Indian and watered in the stream. That was the main reason old Amos was so reluctant to sell any interest in the stream or to the land along its banks when Orson Borden was trying to buy it up. When old Amos finally did sell, he knew what rights he wanted to retain and made sure they were spelled out in detail; he was especially particular in assuring that he, his heirs, and assigns would always have "the right of access to the stream for the use of the water therein for their cattle. . . . "

Things went along without a hitch throughout Orson's ownership in the valley. He well knew what Amos was allowed to do and not do with the stream and the strip of land crossing through the farm. When Frederick succeeded to the estate, no change for the worse was noticeable to the landowners along the stream. He was, in fact, much more tolerant of the uses various owners made of the stream and was far less possessive of the estate than Orson had been.

Amos and Jen moved into the Kirk farmhouse when they married in 1952. A year or two after that, his father and mother decided they had devoted enough of their lives to the land and had endured enough early mornings and late evenings tied down to a herd of cows and set milking times. They sold the farm and stock to Amos and Jen (who paid for it out of her inheritance, which was substantial) and bought a little grocery store in town. Amos never was much on cows. He and Jen were horse people and Holsteins had no place in their future. They sold the herd and converted the dairy barn to stables.

They knew, of course, about the Borden interest in the stream as it ran through the farm and hired Ward Eastman to lay out the lines of the two-hundred-foot-wide strip, one hundred feet on each side of the center. They erected a wood post and rail fence along the lines, mindful not to encroach over onto the Baron's side. They built wide, swinging gates in the fence on both sides of the strip so they could move their horses from the stable area to the pasture on the north side of the stream all in accordance with their "right of way. . .as a means of access to and from the remaining lands of the said first parties. . . ." To continue watering their stock as two generations of Kirks had before them, they built a fence down into the stream at one point on the north side so the horses in pasture could get to the water.

After the upset with the Gagliardis, The Baron studied the deeds to his ownership much more closely than he had before. It was then he discovered that uses were being made of the stream and the land along its banks that were contrary to what the various deeds allowed. Ward Eastman and Gordon Conklin had a busy few years getting all that straightened out to The Baron's satisfaction. They didn't have to build any more fences or take any of the adjoining landowners to court, but The Baron's lines along the stream were well-marked when they were done and the upland owners clearly understood when and for what purpose they could cross those lines. Most of them found out that their rights were far less than what they had been told by the farmers who sold them the land. They cursed The Baron up one side of the stream and down the other and vowed revenge without really saying what form it would take.

When it came to the Kirk place, a new survey wasn't necessary, because the creek still ran in the same location as when Ward had surveyed the lines for Jen and Amos. And they had been careful to keep the fence in good repair so the horses didn't stray to where they didn't belong. But The Baron was sure they were doing something they weren't supposed to. He read the old deed again and again and laughed aloud when he finally discovered what it was. Gordon Conklin was summoned straight-away from Binghamton; he knew not what for until he arrived at the lodge.

"I want you to go down to the Kirk place and tell them to get their damn horses out of my stream and off my land," he was told.

"But they have a right to water their animals in the stream just like they're doing," Gordon advised. "It's all set down in detail in the deed old Amos gave your great-grandfather."

"No, they don't," The Baron retorted. "They have a right to water cattle. They're watering horses and horses aren't cattle. I want them out of there."

Gordon cautioned against it, pointing out that the watering had gone on for years, cows and horses alike. He also reminded The Baron that Amos and Jen depended on that water and without it, they might have to give up the horse farm and go back to dairy farming. If they did that, animals would still be in the stream so what difference did it make what species they were. He counseled The Baron that since Jen was his sister, didn't he think that fostering closer family ties was a good thing.

"She's not my sister, she's my half-sister. Whatever you say, a family member, no matter what her relationship, is due no more privileges than any other owner when she's doing something without a legal right. You stopped all the other prohibited uses up and down the stream, now stop this one." The Baron was adamant, no mistake about that.

"I really think you should approach this one a little differently," Gordon continued to advise. "Perhaps we can work out a lease or a rental arrangement with them. If you insist on going ahead, I'm sure we'll end up in court."

"Yes, I do insist," The Baron said, obviously growing impatient. "I'm not interested in any so-called arrangement. We have a deed and that's all I'll put up with. If you don't want to handle this, I'm sure I can find another attorney who will."

Gordon Conklin was fearful of the havoc another attorney would create up and down the valley, so off he went, reluctantly. Amos and Jen were shocked and angry, Jen the more so. While no love existed between her and The Baron, or between The Baron and any of the rest of the family since he had sent them packing years before, she did hope some sense of family obligation might remain. It didn't, Gordon told her.

Of course, it went to court. Amos and Jen argued that back in the time the deed had been drawn, "cattle" was a generic term commonly used to include all the animals on a farm. (Gordon suggested that position to them, but The Baron was never to know.) The Baron, who had read every stream deed more times than all the rest of the people in the world put together, countered by citing other deeds, when reserving the same right, specified "stock" when it was intended all farm animals could be watered. Gordon did his best to lose the case without being obvious about it, but he didn't. The judge agreed with The Baron and Amos and Jen were ordered to stop watering horses in the stream and to move all of their fence back to the one-hundred-foot line.

They did and had a well drilled on the pasture side of the stream, installed a pump (that was powered by a gasoline motor, because they had no right to run a power line across the stream, The Baron pointed out to them), and built a series of watering troughs. It was a much better setup than the stream watering had been, but that wasn't important to Jen. She had merely hated the Baron before; now, she absolutely detested him. And with good reason, her friends and neighbors in the valley agreed.

When Jen and Amos were married, she was hesitant about moving into the valley and living on a place so near the sites of her treasured childhood memories. But she had spunk and decided that one way she could irritate The Baron was to live next door, so to speak, and ignore him completely. In the four years of her marriage prior to the confrontation over the watering of the horses, she saw him only once. The Baron hardly ever left his property, but on one of those rare occasions when he did, Jen happened to be crossing the road below Hemlock Turn when he drove by. As soon as she realized who it was, she turned her back and stuck her nose in the air. It didn't accomplish much, because The Baron sailed on past without a glance to the right or left. Still, Jen felt better about it and that counted.

Depending on her mood, she was occasionally sorry to reach the farm when she and Amos returned from their trips to horse shows and events around the country. More often she was sorry to leave the valley when they started out for one place or another, a double-horse trailer behind the truck that proudly announced in white letters on both doors "Kirk Horse Farm - Jen & Amos Kirk."

Sometimes she was mad and other times she was sad. The sad times were sure to come if she rode up to the parking lot at the end of the town road and passed the fishing hole on the stream that had been Nicky's favorite. After the leaves fell from the trees in the fall, she could catch a glimpse of the old ski jump up the deep hollow off to the south of the road. She wondered if The Baron had destroyed the glider or if it was still there in the garage where her grandfather, the chauffeur, and the handyman had taken it after it finally fell from the top of the big spruce tree. She thought a lot about Nicky when she went up the valley. She had been close to him—closer than she was to Linc, who always seemed so distant, or to Jack, who said he just didn't like girls. (When he reached his late teens, that all changed.) Nicky had been five years older than Jen and he was the one who looked out for her and protected her as she grew. He was her best friend, she had often told him, and the one she confided in when she had a secret to tell.

They never really knew what happened to Nicky. He and his 'plane had disappeared behind enemy lines north of Seoul in the spring of 1951. They hoped he had survived as a prisoner of war, even with all the negative aspects of that fate. When the North Koreans finally agreed to the exchange of prisoners in April of 1953 that became known as Operation Little Switch, they were confident he would appear. A total of 149 Americans were released by the North Korean and Chinese Communist forces during that exchange, but

Nicky wasn't one of them. Between August 5 and September 6, 1953, just after the Korean War ended, another 3,597 Americans were released in a second prisoner exchange called Operation Big Switch. Nicky was not one of those either. And so he remained one of the 8,177 Americans listed as "missing in action" at the end of the Korean War and ever after. It was as much for Nicky as for herself that Jen decided to make her home with Amos on the old Kirk place along Indian Brook.

However, the others were also devastated by the two major tragedies in their lives. Of course the deaths of their father and their grandfather were tragedies, too, but they seemed better able to understand those. Frederick was along in years when he died so his passing was not unexpected. And they had been an ocean away when their father was killed in the early days of World War II. But they had grown up with Nicky on the vast estate there in the Catskills. To lose one was bad enough; to lose both was heart-wrenching.

They survived though and went on to better things, never forgetting, however, the days, the places, and the people of those happy times of youth. Linc never did enlist in the Tenth Mountain Division. The war was nearly over when he came of age and his grandfather sent him off to Harvard. He was graduated in the top ten percent of his class and entered the diplomatic corps of the State Department. In time, he moved over to the United Nations and was still there, part of his duties requiring him to travel to various trouble spots around the world. He was off on one of those junkets when word of The Baron's death reached him.

Jack's love for boats and ships and the sea never abated. He, too, missed World War II and was at Annapolis during the Korean War. He rose quickly in the navy, being at the rank of commander in 1964. His duty station was aboard a battleship of the Atlantic Fleet with home port at Norfolk, Virginia. He was at sea much of the time, but was in port when The Baron was murdered.

The Mouse was a sad case. Jessie had taken her back to France in 1951, after Nicky had been declared missing. She was then in her late teens and still possessed the dreamy qualities that characterized her early years. She met her husband, then a captain in the French army and some ten years her senior, not long after she and Jessie arrived in Paris. She was deeply in love with him she told her mother. Jessie tried to discourage the relationship because of the whispered tales she heard about the captain and his liaisons with this woman and that, married and otherwise. But The Mouse was not to be deterred and she and the captain were wed in 1953, when she was just nineteen.

The captain didn't take to married life (his own, that is) and continued his philandering ways. The Mouse took to drink and slowly, but surely, descended into the depths of alcoholism. The captain was finally discharged from the army—cashiered, some said, for conduct unbecoming an officer, although his discharge stated it was honorable. Through some connection or another, he got himself appointed to the French delegation at the United Nations. He and The Mouse traveled back and forth between Paris and New York, she not much caring which side of the Atlantic they were on. They were on the New York side when the pistol shots were fired in the cabin at the head of the Indian.

11.
Friday, December 4, 1964 -
Sunday, September 5, 1965

THE FIELDWORK of the Borden survey continued off and on throughout the winter and was nearly finished as spring drew closer. All the boundary line that remained to be run was two miles along the division line between Great Lots 7 and 8. The southeasterly one mile or so was common with state land in Great Lot 8 and the remainder ran along private land over in Walker Hollow on the northerly slopes of Hawk Mountain. Much of the two miles was off on the back side of Hawk and Indian mountains and was remote and difficult to reach, requiring a long walk regardless of where the approach hike was begun. Ward Eastman knew the running would be good; he had been on the state land part of the line some thirty years before. The woods had been open then—even the stunted growth at the higher elevations—and most shots were about four chains long. He didn't expect conditions had changed over the years; if anything, the line along the state land portion would probably be more open because these lands were part of the Catskill Forest Preserve where no tree cutting was allowed.

They spent the first week in March marking and painting the final lines on the Bush farm. The snow still covered the ground there to a depth of a foot or two on the northerly slopes and they went on snowshoes most of the time. The snow was quickly turning to spring conditions—corn snow, it was called, being granular and coarse like kernels of corn—but it would have been a tough slog without the greater area of the webbed shoes to distribute the weight of the walker over a wider surface. By Friday, all that was left to do was set the corners down along the Schoharie and around the two house lots that had been sold off the farm. That was a two-man job, so Ward decided to leave it to Bruce and Steve while he scouted out the two miles of the Borden boundary up on Hawk and Indian.

He headed for the line by way of Indian Brook Valley and drove to the parking lot at the end of the town road, leaving the pickup truck parked there. He now had a key to the gate—and to all the other gates on the property as well. Lincoln Borden had been far more understanding about that than The Baron had been. However, the road from the gate to the cabin wasn't plowed in the winter and Ward knew some deep patches of snow would remain to make the road a difficult and chancy drive. The days were warmer now and the melting snow would have turned some low spots into mud holes. He didn't want to suffer the same fate the phalanx of police officials had the preceding fall.

He strapped his snowshoes to the back of his pack; he was sure he wouldn't need them low down in the valley, but he expected to find deeper snow higher up. He shouldered his pack, which held his lunch and two one-pint water jugs together with a fifty-foot tape, a pancho, a sweater, and an extra pair of gloves. He patted his jacket pocket to make sure he had his compass and the maps of the state land survey from thirty years ago. He picked up his double-bitted cruiser's ax and started up the woods road.

The walk to the cabin went swiftly. When he came to drifts of snow or muddy spots, he detoured off the road into the woods. For the most part, however, he was able to keep to the high part in the center between the two wheel tracks. The cabin looked the same; he supposed the blood had been cleaned from the floor and noticed the broken window was boarded over. Ward stopped in back of the cabin and rested a few minutes sitting on the same rock where he and Steve had waited for Bruce to return with the police that late afternoon in October of the previous fall.

He hiked up the old trail that ran to the saddle between Twin and Indian. He had walked it a number of times back in the days when it was open to the public; in fact, it was the trail he had used as one of the approaches to the survey of thirty years before. The corner of the state land, where the line of it turned northeasterly into Great Lot 8, was a large truncated rock an early surveyor had christened "Pyramid Rock." The name had stuck and every surveyor thereafter, when describing that corner, referred to it as Pyramid Rock. It didn't really look like a pyramid and Ward always wondered if that surveyor had selected it because his bearing and distance brought him there or because it was so distinctive. He was sure it was the latter because other early surveyors, running the same line, weren't anywhere near it when they passed by. William Cockburn, in 1784, put the line nearly thirteen chains northeasterly of the rock. William Martin, on his 1892 survey, was well over two chains southwest of the rock. However, John B. Davis, in 1846, said the rock was on the line between Great Lots 7 and 8 and that it marked the corner of two tracts in Great Lot 8. It was Davis who gave it the sobriquet "Pyramid Rock" and all the surveyors who followed (except Martin, of course) accepted it as the corner.

Ward knew he could reach the rock by branching left when he was about halfway up the trail between the cabin and the saddle. As best he could remember, it was about 300 or 400 feet off the trail. The woods were quite open at that point and he was sure he would recognize the spot. He didn't—after all, it had been thirty years ago—but when he sensed he was somewhere near the right place, he moved across the slope toward a clump of spruce trees he could see beyond the tall hardwoods nearer the trail. As he drew closer, he saw that the spruces, which were about eight feet tall, hid the rock. There it was, just as he remembered it. "Not bad for an old-timer," he said aloud, congratulating himself on being able to walk to it after all those years.

Since it was not quite ten o'clock, he decided to scout out the one mile of common state/Borden boundary line that ran southeasterly from the rock. Although he didn't see any of the yellow paint the forest rangers used on the tree blazes along the state land boundaries, he did see some old marks running northeast and southeast out from the rock. These were the blazes he had made along the line thirty years ago and would be easy to follow even if they weren't painted. He thought he could probably cover the one mile and be back by noon or soon thereafter, so he took off his pack and left it beside the rock. He hadn't yet needed the snowshoes, so he left them behind also, although he suspected he would encounter some deep snow here and there once he got over on the north side of Indian Mountain.

The going was good and the marks easy to pick up. He cut off some low-hanging branches and beech saplings in the line as he moved swiftly along, blazing a few trees here and there. It was only half-past-eleven when he reached the pile of stones that marked the back corner of the Borden lands. The transit station they had set beside it last fall was still there, the tack still firm in the top of it. He decided the best way to run the mile of line would be to chop it out and set transit stations from Pyramid Rock to the pile of stones and, then, run the traverse on the way back. It would be a long day, but he thought the three of them could make it before dark.

The trek back to Pyramid Rock went quickly. He cut some more brush on the way so they would have less to do when they came to actually run the line. The sun had disappeared before he reached the pile of stones and heavy, dark clouds now moved across the sky. By the time he came in sight of the rock, large, wet snowflakes were falling and sticking to the limbs of the trees. "Sap snow" his grandfather had called these thick squalls that came in late winter during maple syrup time. When they came in the early spring and covered the open fields, they were then the "poor man's fertilizer." The storms usually didn't last long, but could be really uncomfortable if they changed over to rain.

His pack and snowshoes were covered with an inch of snow when he reached them. The sky was still a dark gray and the snow didn't seem to be letting up. If he wanted a dry lunch, he realized he'd have to find some shelter. The rock itself leaned toward the spruce trees and under this overhang and the thick limbs of the trees he found a protected spot. He stripped sheets of bark from a gray birch and broke off some twigs and limbs from a dead spruce. Might as well have a fire while I'm at it, he resolved. He looked around for a small beech sapling of just the right shape and, with a few deft strokes of his ax, fashioned it into a long-handled fork, ideal for holding his sandwich over an open fire. The old-time survey crews had always carried a tea pail and boiled up two or three brews over a roaring fire at every lunch time. But that tradition had faded away and he would have to be satisfied with a toasted sandwich.

He crawled under the spruce trees and into the small clearing under the rock. He laid the birch bark and twigs in a pile off to one side so the wind would blow the smoke of the fire away from him although he knew that if the fire began to smolder, the wind would shift to blow the smoke directly in his face. It always did. He needed only one match to start a small flame curling up from the bark. As it grew and caught the twigs, he broke off the lower dead branches from the nearest spruce and added them, in short lengths, to the fire. Warmth soon filled the tiny clearing. He let the fire burn down to coals before toasting his sandwich—coals made toast, open flames only burned and blackened the bread.

The snow, with occasional spits of rain, continued after he had finished his lunch. He decided to wait for it to stop or, at least, let up. He broke off some more spruce branches and built the fire back up. He pulled his pipe and tobacco pouch from the pocket of his wool shirt and put together a smoke. He leaned back against the rock and contentedly watched the smoke drift up from his pipe. As the fire died down, he added more wood to it using dead twigs that lay scattered about the little clearing and under the leaning rock. The sky turned darker and darker and the snow changed to rain. Looks like it's not going to clear, he mused, but elected to stay put a while longer.

He kept the fire going, but soon ran low on a supply of wood. He noticed some larger twigs back under the rock and, using his toasting stick, worked them out to where he could reach them. As he searched further, his stick hit something that didn't move and he thought it probably a stone wedged under the rock. He bent down to see what it was and if more sticks might be off to one side. As he did, the fire flared up in a gust of wind and lit the small clearing and the space under the rock. Ward saw the object wasn't a stone at all and, maneuvering his stick behind it, slowly drew it out into the clearing.

It was a pistol. He was no expert on guns, but he did recognize this one was the same caliber and make as the one in the display box that hung next to The Baron's desk at the lodge. He looked more closely and saw it was inscribed "U.S. Army - United States Property." He remembered that the one at the lodge had the same inscription. He was sure he held the pistol missing from the pair and that it was the murder weapon. He had been right, after all, in suggesting to Morrissy and Burgin that the killer had come into and gone out of the valley by the old foot trail. He realized this very spot was probably where he had spent the night prior to the murder. He looked carefully around the small clearing and under the rock for some other sign—a food wrapper, remains of a fire, a cigarette butt, anything—indicating that someone had camped here. He found nothing. The pistol was all that had been left behind and that obviously had been hidden. At least whoever had put it there had thought it was hidden.

He held the pistol with his gloves on so as not to smudge any fingerprints—although he doubted it still held any—and put it in his pack. It probably had bullets remaining in the clip; he remembered that only two had been fired in the cabin. He pushed the pack out of the clearing and scooped snow over the fire to put it out, even though it probably wouldn't spread as wet as everything was becoming in the continuing rain. He couldn't wait for clear weather any longer; he had to get to Milltown and the police barracks as soon as possible. Well, that really didn't make much sense, he reasoned; since the pistol had lain under the rock for six months or so, another few hours wasn't going to make any difference. He tied the snowshoes on the pack, shouldered it, picked up his ax, and hurried across the slope to the trail.

As he hiked down the mountain and past the cabin, one thought kept running through his mind. Whoever it was, he sure knew his way around the trails and backwoods of the Borden lands. He hadn't come on that ready-made shelter of the rock and spruce trees by chance. It was too far off the trail for that. He—or she, he corrected himself—knew it was there. The murderer was no stranger; he was as sure of that now as he had been all along. If only he could figure out how The Baron had been lured to the cabin that morning, he might have all the answers.

Contrary to what Ward had expected, his finding the pistol didn't cause much excitement. Burgin wasn't at the barracks when he arrived in the late afternoon, so he left it with the officer on duty at the desk, who put it in a glassine envelope and took down information about where, when, and how it had been found. He thought he might hear from someone in a day or two and be asked to guide some investigators to the site so they might conduct their own search of the area. But no summons came.

It wasn't until five or six weeks later that he ran into Burgin while both were stopped for gas at Tom Smythe's Sunoco station.

"What did you find out about the pistol I brought in?" Ward asked after they had exchanged the usual pleasantries of meeting.

"Oh, it was the murder weapon, all right. The ballistics lab up in Albany confirmed that. And it was the missing one of the matched pair that belonged to Borden. A Colt, government model 1911A1, .45 caliber, it was. Held a seven-shot clip of which two had been fired. The pistol we found in the lodge was fully loaded. Guess he kept them that way. You'll remember the butler said Borden used them for target shooting on a regular basis."

"Did it help any in your investigation?" Ward questioned.

"Not that you'd notice," Burgin replied. "It's just one small piece in a big jigsaw puzzle. We've got a lot more pieces to fit in before we can figure out what the final picture will look like."

Ward caught the simile. It was obvious, however, that Burgin still didn't appreciate the importance of the location where the pistol had been hidden. Over the past few weeks, he, Bruce, and Steve had spent a number of days up on the slopes of Hawk and Indian mountains in the vicinity of Pyramid Rock. They hadn't seen anyone around the rock or any tracks in the snow nearby. It was clear the police hadn't visited the site. Probably too far off the road, Ward concluded disgustedly. Well, that was their business, not his. He'd found the pistol, what they did with it after that was up to them.

Ward had a call from Lincoln Borden over the Memorial Day weekend. (Memorial Day was on a Sunday that year.) He told him the entire family would be in the valley over the coming Labor Day holiday and they all hoped the final map would be completed by then so they might go over it in some detail and reach decisions about partitioning the property. It was a tight time schedule because the map would have to be a large one consisting of many sheets, but Ward assured him that it would be ready. That settled, it was left that Ward would call at the lodge at 1:00 PM on Sunday, September 5.

The date seemed a long way off, but the computations yet to be done were extensive and all three worked on the mapping. Rainy days weren't so bad, but they regretted watching the good days of summer drift by the open windows of the office. The weeks went by quickly and so did the map work. In the end, it consisted of fifteen sheets that, if joined together, formed an overall map measuring nine feet by ten feet. They printed six full sets that Ward rolled separately and put on the seat of the truck beside him as he drove off to keep his appointment. The survey had been a long time in the making, but it was done; all the boundary lines were blazed and painted with red paint, all the corners were monumented, for the most part with piles of stones, some found during the course of the survey and others set to replace those that were missing. The map was done; it depicted all the roads, trails, buildings, streams, and other important physical features in addition to the boundaries and corners. Ward was well-satisfied with what they had accomplished. The family members were all at the lodge at the appointed hour and Ward was finally able to fit faces with familiar names and to match husbands and wives. They were pleasant, both individually and together; the contrast between them and The Baron was remarkable. He had never sought Ward's advise about anything and became irritated if it was offered. These Bordens, however, asked questions, listened to the answers, and appreciated Ward's suggestions, many of which they followed.

It was a long afternoon, but the time spent was agreeable and even relaxing. By the end of the session, they had decided how to divide the property and who would have which buildings and what land. Ward was retained to survey the partition lines and to prepare a separate map of each of the resulting segments. How the division would be handled within the confines of Orson Borden's will, Ward didn't fully understand, but suspected it would be through some form of lease made effective for only the lifetime of the leasee. That was Gordon Conklin's field of battle and Ward was happy to leave it to him.

The discussion took place in the den—it was the only room large enough to hold the fully joined map and all members of the family grouped around it. Ward couldn't help but notice that the key board and the pistol display box were no longer there. Once all the decisions had been made and Ward had made notes of them, the maps were rolled and Ward carried them and his other papers out to the truck.

They asked him to stay for a time and join them out on the lawn down by the pond. It had been a family tradition, Lincoln explained, before The Baron succeeded to the property, for them to gather on the Sunday of the Labor Day holiday weekend for drinks and hors d'oeuvres and to toast the summer past and those summers yet to come. Ward accepted; it would be a fitting way to conclude the most extensive survey he had ever been involved with.

They walked across the wide lawn to the summerhouse that sat back from the pond. Servants had laid out the food in a buffet setting in the summer house and had one long table well-stocked with bottles and glasses and ice buckets. One man, obviously ready to fulfill the role of bartender, stood by the table prepared to fix drinks or to assist those who wished to pour their own. Once everyone had a full glass, Lincoln raised his and thanked the Deity for the summer and, especially, for returning the property so they could enjoy it once again. The rest raised their glasses, too, and said simply "Amen."

Ward thought he would feel out of place in the gathering, but he didn't. They were gracious hosts and included him in their conversations. They were interested in the details of the survey and his descriptions of the work and how they had carried it through in all kinds of weather, fair and foul, winter and summer. The food was good and the drinks were cold—Ward had vodka and tonic in a tall glass; he had yet to drive home, so made it last. He noticed the one they called The Mouse didn't make her drinks last. She sat, half-reclined, in a lawn chair next to the summerhouse and raised her glass high when it was empty as a summons to her husband, the captain, who dutifully saw that it was filled.

As the afternoon waned, Ward decided he had stayed his welcome and circulated from person to person saying his good-byes. He was talking with Lincoln, confirming some last details about the partition survey when they heard the sound of an airplane motor approaching from down the valley. The 'plane came slowly into view and all stopped talking to watch it. It was of World War I vintage, a biplane with a single cockpit and the tail rudder embellished with three vertical stripes of red, white, and blue. It swooped over the pond so low they could see the pilot. He wore a leather flying helmet with the goggles pulled down over his eyes. A long, white scarf was wrapped around his neck and trailed in the wind out over the fuselage of the 'plane. They were fascinated and watched as the airplane circled once over the pond and then gained in altitude as it headed for the gap between Twin and Indian mountains.

"Shades of the past," proclaimed The Mouse as she raised her glass and twirled it 'round and 'round so the ice cubes in it tinkled a signal to the captain that it was time for another refill.

That broke the spell and the conversations picked up where they had been left off. Ward took his leave from Lincoln and walked across the lawn toward his truck. The airplane was just disappearing off in the distance as he stopped and glanced back at the family group. He looked from one to another, studying each face. He knew who the murderer was.

12.
Spring, 1951 -
Sunday, September 5, 1965

1ST LT. NICHOLAS A. BORDEN was not happy. Oh, sure, he was piloting an airplane, but he really belonged in one of those F-80 Shooting Star jets the Air Force had or, maybe, an F9F Panther the Marines were flying. Instead, here he was puddle-jumping along in a Stinson OY Grasshopper spotting for I Corps G2 (Intelligence) with an occasional artillery mission thrown in for variety. He was qualified in jets and continually sought a transfer, but always received the same answer, "That's for the Air Force, we've got other things to do."

His commanding officer tried to soothe the lieutenant's irritation with praise, "No one else can fly that Grasshopper like you do. No one else gets that close to what we need to know about and comes out unscathed."

"Unscathed, hell," 1st Lt. Nicholas A. Borden thought to himself. "I never come back from a mission without bullet holes through the wings or the windows shot up. Look how many times I've landed in some rice paddy because the motor was hit and conked out before I could get back to the field." But he didn't speak his thoughts aloud when others were around because a compliment was a compliment and good to hear. He was a good pilot and he knew it. The only mishap he had ever had that resulted from his own bad judgment was when he put that glider up in the top of the old spruce tree.

What bothered him as much as anything was that the Grasshopper carried no armament. He was continually being shot at, but couldn't shoot back. He did have his .45, however; all officers were issued one of those. He scrounged another one from the quartermaster and talked the Turkish Brigade out of a bucket of hand grenades. He kept both .45s loaded and stuck down in the side pocket of his seat along with his maps and looked for targets of opportunity. He dipped low over enemy trucks and dropped hand grenades; they usually exploded before they reached the ground. He fired his .45s out the side window at troops below; they, however, returned the fire with rifles and tallied far more hits on him than he did on them.

Finally, one day in early May, he did score a bull's-eye. He spotted a jeep racing down an empty stretch of road deep in enemy territory with only the driver and an officer as passengers. 1st Lt. Nicholas A. Borden opened the side windows of his Grasshopper and swooped down over the jeep. It picked up speed; Nicky throttled back to match its pace. He dipped to about fifty feet above the road and began to drop grenades, one by one. Just as the road turned to cross the bridge over a wide river, one of Nicky's grenades struck beside the left front wheel and blew the tire. The jeep swerved out of control, missed the bridge, plunged down the embankment, and disappeared into the water below. Nicky pulled up and circled the spot a few times; nothing moved but the water of the river. It was a clean kill. In his report for the day, he boasted, "Sighted jeep, sank same."

The whole war (It wasn't a war. Official Washington corrected any who said so; it was a police action.) was frustrating. First it was down the Korean peninsula; then, it was up the peninsula; and, then, down again. Up, down, up, down. It would never end, he and many others had come to believe. When the People's Liberation Army entered the war in late 1950, the Allied Command started numbering the Chinese advances. The Third Chinese Offensive pushed the front lines south of Seoul in early January of 1951 and South Korea's capitol city fell for the second time. Nicky didn't know what the First and Second Chinese offensives had accomplished; they had taken place before he reached the Land of the Morning Calm. The Fourth Chinese Offensive was in February, the Fifth was in April, the Sixth was in May and on it went.

Each drive north by the United Nations forces was also given a name: Operation Killer, Operation Ripper, Operation Thunderbolt, Operation Roundup, or some other gruesome title designed to bolster support and the confidence of the American people. However, the facts were that the only Americans who cared were those who had loved ones embroiled in the fighting; the rest didn't know a war (Sorry, police action.) was going on. Now, here we are, Nicky speculated, trying to push back the latest Chinese offensive and next week we'll probably be heading south again. No, 1st Lt. Nicholas A. Borden wasn't happy. "War is hell," William Tecumseh Sherman had said and he was right.

The line on that morning in late May of 1951 ran well north of Seoul to the Imjin River. Nicky's mission was to fly north of the river, west past Kaesong, and toward the Ongjin Peninsula, the isolated western outpost of South Korea. His orders that morning were to scout for enemy troop concentrations and to be on the lookout for any movement of trucks or other supply trains. It was a routine mission and he had flown the route before. That was the point—what he spotted on this day could be compared with the report of his flight of the week before and the changes could be readily noted to guide those who planned the next day's or week's operation. He pulled up over a low ridge and dropped down the far side.

Just as he cleared the military crest on the back side of the ridge, the motor sputtered and a row of holes was stitched across the cabin floor. Next, his right foot felt as if it had been hit by a sledgehammer and the flesh of his thigh seemed to erupt. Blood spattered his face and sprayed on the roof of the cabin. He realized that a burp gun fired by a North Korean (Or a Chinaman, who was to know?) out of an enemy mortar emplacement had caught the Grasshopper and left its mark in a neat line from engine to tail. Two of the bullets—or maybe three—had passed upward through his right foot and leg.

He pulled back on the stick, trying to force the faltering airplane to gain altitude. He jiggled the throttle; the motor coughed, sputtered, and settled down to an even hum and, then, coughed again. He banked to the left, flying west. He knew from the way the motor was acting he couldn't reach his base back below the Imjin. He didn't relish the thought of coming down behind enemy lines and ending up as a prisoner of war for months—or maybe years, the way the war was going.

He'd heard that South Korean guerrillas occupied some of the small islands off the coast of the Ongjin Peninsula and that British commandos sometimes used them as a base from which they conducted raids on enemy positions on the mainland. If he could reach the open water of the Yellow Sea, maybe he could set the 'plane down near one of those islands and make it to shore. If the Grasshopper got that far, that is.

The motor died, sputtered twice, then caught again. Nicky was sure it was a problem with the fuel line, but had no way of setting it right. His leg was numb and blood covered the seat and ran down the floor of the cabin. He fashioned a tourniquet with his belt to stop the blood pulsing out of the wound in his thigh. He coaxed the 'plane along—it dropped quickly each time the motor quit. When it caught again, he pulled up and struggled to gain the lost altitude. In time, he reached the open water and picked out a likely island—the one he could see farthest from the mainland—and headed for it. The motor quit again and nothing he did brought it back to life. He tried to hold the Grasshopper in a glide, pointing toward the island. However, with a useless right leg, he had trouble keeping the 'plane level and, to add to his problems, his eyes wouldn't focus. Must be loss of blood, he concluded. As he was about to pancake on the water, he momentarily lost control; the right wing dipped and caught the water surface. The 'plane cartwheeled, came to rest upside down, and slowly began to sink.

1st Lt. Nicholas A. Borden never knew what really happened then or over the next couple of weeks. The pilot's seat had been snapped loose when the Grasshopper hit and he was thrown about the cabin. He smashed his head, wrenched his left shoulder, and a long gash was ripped down his back. He drifted in and out of consciousness and could later recall only bits and pieces of events. He remembered being dragged from the 'plane by people who spoke a language other than English. Next—how much later, he didn't know—he felt himself being carried by men who did speak English, although with a decided British accent. Then, he heard the sound of a motor—an outboard, he thought—and felt the roll of water beneath him.

The first clear sensation he had was lying on something soft and the feel and smell of clean sheets. As he opened his eyes to look at his surroundings, he was startled to see the face of a woman—a plain face, but a pretty face and a smiling one. Her name was Jane, she said, Jane Holligan. She explained that she was a Red Cross volunteer from

England and they were on the Danish hospital ship Jutlandia somewhere off the coast of South Korea. He was going to live, she told
him, but he was badly banged up and it would be some time before
he was mended enough to get about. The doctors had been able to
save his right leg and, while he would eventually be able to walk, they
doubted he'd ever lose the limp that would result from the damage
to his foot.

He soon found out the big question in everyone's mind was, who
was he? His dog tags were missing and he carried no other identifica-
tion. The Brits who had brought him to the hospital ship could
provide no information about how long he had been on the island
where they had discovered him or how he had gotten there to begin
with. They found him one morning just outside their camp lying on
a makeshift stretcher, crudely bandaged, and dressed in Korean
clothes.

As Jane was telling the story, Nicky decided to feign amnesia. He
didn't really know why, but he did know he'd had enough of war
and maybe this was how he could get out of it for good. He was also
not happy with the path his life had taken before the war and maybe
here was a ready-made opportunity to start living anew.

What followed was a long story and it was a long journey from
there to the cabin at the head of the Indian. For much of the way, he
and Jane traveled it together. He had confided in her almost from the
first and she kept his secret. Once he was up and getting around with
Jane's help, they left the ship when it docked at Kobe, Japan, and
never returned. They took a roundabout route to her home near
Coventry in the Midlands and were married. He gave himself a new
name, Colin Taylor, and, in time, took out British citizenship. But
he yearned for home and, in the late 1950s, he and Jane immigrated
to the United States and settled in Pennsylvania.

He thought about his mother and his brothers and sisters and
wished he could see them and let them know he was alive and well.
But he was a deserter as far as the United States government was
concerned and 1st Lt. Nicholas A. Borden was better left as missing.
From time to time, he saw mention of Jen and followed her equestrian
achievements through accounts in the newspapers. Once he and Jane
went to a jumping exhibition in Philadelphia and watched as Jen and
Amos rode the course. He desperately wanted to go down and talk
to her, but kept his seat in the stands.

As the years passed, he longed more and more to visit the Catskills' property. He wondered if The Baron was still there and if Jen and Linc, Jack and The Mouse, and Jessie were still unwelcome. He finally decided to find out. He would see the property and answer the questions about his family at the same time. He told Jane of his plan and she asked to be a part of it, but understood when Nicky explained why he had to go alone. So it was that he parked the rental car in the trailhead parking lot just off the county road along the West Branch of the Neversink on the morning of Sunday, September 6, 1964, the day before Labor Day.

The last, long-holiday weekend of the season was a popular one for day hikers in the Catskills and Nicky was not surprised to find a number of cars parked there when he arrived. All the better, he could blend with the crowd and his face would be less memorable by being one of many. He hiked the Breadloaf Brook trail up to the saddle between Twin and Indian mountains. All the therapy and exercise he had put his leg and foot through over the years had restored much of the use of them and he was able to move steadily along.

When he reached the saddle, he saw the posted signs marking the height of land clearly stating that he and the rest of the world were not wanted down the Indian Brook side of the mountain. He spotted the figure of a man skulking furtively in the underbrush off the trail. Aha, thought Nicky, so The Baron has a watch-dog. He paused at the trail junction, pulled a trail map from his pocket and scanned it, looking up at the trails to the right and to the left. He folded the map, stuffed it back in his pocket and turned left, taking the trail to Twin. If the watch-dog was observing him and he was sure he was, Nicky didn't want his actions to appear any different than other hiker out for the day and climbing the Catskills' high peaks.

He continued climbing up the trail for some distance before beginning to drop down the mountain. He kept descending until he could see the horse trail that led from the lodge to the hunting cabin at the head of Indian Brook. He stayed in the woods above the trail, out of the sight of anyone who might be using it. Quietly, slowly, and carefully, he worked his way along to a point above the pond and directly across from the lodge. He remembered the small ledge where he used to come to read on warm summer days long ago. He could see the lodge from there and the wide lawn that sloped down past the summerhouse to the water's edge. If his brothers and sisters and his mother were to be at the lodge, this was the time. They all had looked forward to the picnic at the end of the summer on this afternoon of every year. It was a family tradition. He knew they would keep it, if it was possible for them to do so.

The top of the ledge had grown over with tangled shrubs of witch hopple since he had last been to it. He took off the small day-pack he carried and placed it next to a beech tree that grew back from the ledge. He sat on the soft, warm ground and leaned back against the tree. He could see the shimmer of the lake, the green of the lawn, and the lodge from his perch. He had purposely worn dark clothes so he would better merge with the leaves of the trees and the brush of the deep woods. Seated as he was behind the witch hopple, and blending with the green in front and in back of where he sat, he knew he was invisible to anyone who might look this way from the lodge. He took a pair of field glasses out of his pack and settled himself comfortably. It was just after one o'clock. If the end-of-the-year picnic was to be held, people should soon start to arrive.

The afternoon dragged on. All was quiet at the lodge. Nothing moved down there. Not much moved where Nicky was either except now and then a blue jay landed on the limbs of the beech and squawked at him. He heard squirrels chattering and scurrying about through the brush and once a chipmunk ran over his foot not realizing he wasn't part of the landscape.

Occasionally, he scanned the lawn and the windows of the lodge through his field glasses. He saw no movement or sign of life until a little after four. Then a man came out of the lodge and walked across the lawn toward the dock that reached out into the pond just below the summerhouse. Nicky watched him through the glasses. Although it had been years since he had seen The Baron, he recognized that's who it was. He stood on the end of the dock and smoked a cigarette while looking down into the water and across the pond to the mountains beyond. After a few minutes, he flicked the cigarette into the pond and strode back across the lawn to the pickup truck that was parked next to the back door of the lodge. The truck roared into life and The Baron drove down the driveway across the outlet of the pond and disappeared off in the distance.

It was obvious to Nicky then—and had been almost since he had first reached his stand—that no picnic was going to be held that day. It was also obvious that The Baron was still king of his castle and the rest of the family were outcasts. He replaced the field glasses in the pack and swung it onto his back. Still being cautious, he climbed straight up the slope behind the ledge and intersected the state trail high up near the top of Twin Mountain. He descended the trail to the parking lot, reaching his car just about dusk. He drove off, troubled in his mind and wondering how—or if—he could set things right.

In the weeks that followed, he formulated and discarded a number of plans. They each ended at a single point; he had to confront The Baron. That, however, included the danger of revealing himself. Nicky knew that once The Baron found out he was alive, he would surely turn him in to the authorities and his life thereafter would be unbearable. If The Baron had a card to play, he'd play it, no mistake about that. Unless, of course, Nicky held a trump card.

He didn't tell Jane that he was contemplating another trip to the Catskills because he wasn't sure what the result would be and he didn't want to worry her beforehand. In mid-October, she received word that her mother had been badly injured in a motoring accident and was asking for her. Jane left for England as soon as the trip could be arranged with no idea how long before she would return. That cleared the last obstacle in the way of Nicky's plan. He wrote the note before leaving for the valley of the Indian. "Dear Barron," it said;

> As you see, I'm alive after all. In my travels about the world after my "death," I spent considerable time in Germany. While there, I ran into old friends and acquaintances of our father and your mother. I believe you must know that you have an older half-brother who still lives there. On the other hand, he obviously doesn't know the complete story of his paternal heritage and that he is entitled to the legacy you have claimed. Will be at the cabin at 9:00 AM. Want to see you about this matter of extreme importance.
>
> Your brother, Nicky.

It was mid-afternoon on Tuesday, October 20, 1964, when Nicky left the rental car in the parking lot over on the West Branch. Only one car was there before him. The hiking season was over and the big-game hunting season hadn't yet started; the woods and trails would be empty. He climbed the Breadloaf Brook trail and turned right at the saddle, heading for the summit of Indian Mountain. He scanned the woods carefully as he climbed, alert for some sight or other sign of the watcher he had seen on his earlier trip. He was alone this time, however, and had the woods all to himself.

He left the trail and moved down the slope of the mountain looking for the large rock he had camped beside a number of times in those happy days when his grandfather had owned the property. Although it had been years since he had been to the site, his course was unerring and the rock soon loomed up ahead. A number of spruce trees had grown up on the lower side of the rock since his last visit. All the better, he thought, they would help hide the spot where he planned to spend the night or, at least, part of the night.

He crawled in under the lower limbs of the spruces pulling his pack along behind. It was just as he remembered; a small, flat clearing extended under the leaning rock. It was here that he had camped so many times before. He spread out his sleeping bag and emptied his pack of the portable stove, water bottles, and cans of food he had brought along. He prepared his supper and, after eating it, lay on top of the sleeping bag to rest until dark. He had miles to go before morning.

It was a full moon that night; he had made sure it would be before settling on a final schedule. The obscure light filtered down through the trees casting long and eerie shadows. He picked his way slowly across the slope; now was not the time to break a leg or sprain an ankle. He had walked over to the old trail to make sure he could still find it when first he had reached the rock. Now he gained it again and walked downhill toward the cabin.

The cabin was much larger than he remembered. Must be The Baron had either added onto the old one or had built a new one. Putting on a pair of thin gloves, he tried the doors and windows. All were locked.

The old horse trail was wide and easy to follow even in the uncertain dark of the moonlit night. He carried a flashlight, but didn't want to use it if he could get along without it. In time, he saw the lights of the lodge through the trees. He approached it cautiously. He hadn't seen or heard any dogs when he had watched the lodge those few weeks ago, so he thought none would be around now to announce his presence.

He could see into the lighted den when he reached the bridge crossing the outlet of the pond. The Baron was there, working at his desk. Nicky sat on the low stone railing on the side of the bridge and waited. At eleven o'clock, The Baron rose from the desk and turned out the lights. A few minutes later, lights went on in the large front bedroom upstairs. Nicky waited. About midnight, the upstairs lights went out and the lodge was completely dark. Still he waited.

It was two o'clock when Nicky moved stealthily across to the large maple tree that grew in the middle of the wide lawn. He reached up into the gaping knothole and smiled when his fingers touched the metal ring that hung on the nail at the back. The key still fit the lock on the back door. He slowly—very slowly—turned it, and then the door knob, after the lock pulled back. He expected the furniture would be placed differently than it had been years ago, so he used the flashlight to wend his way through to the den. He had put black tape over the lens, leaving only a thin sliver of light to beam through and even that he kept partially covered with his gloved fingers.

He laid the note in the middle of the desk, where The Baron would be sure to see it. He moved the light around the room and saw the display box of pistols and the board of keys. He took one of the keys from the hook labeled "Cabin." Why wait outside when he got there if he could be more comfortable inside, he reasoned.

He locked the door of the lodge and returned the large key ring to its place at the back of the knothole. It was nearly five o'clock when he zipped up his sleeping bag at the camp under the rock. He had time for an hour or two of sleep before the next step in his plan.

He reached the cabin just after eight o'clock and used the key to let himself in. It was cold inside and he busied himself building a blazing fire in the fireplace. The cabin soon warmed and Nicky sat on the couch, stretching his legs toward the fire. He had nearly dropped off to sleep when he heard the pickup truck coming up the road. It jolted to a halt in front of the cabin and, short seconds later, the door of the cabin was flung open. The greeting was not formal.

"Just what the hell are you talking about? I don't have an older brother," The Baron yelled as he slapped Nicky's note down on the desk.

The conversation went downhill from there. Actually, it wasn't much of a conversation. It consisted mostly of The Baron ranting and raving. He cursed Nicky and his mother and his brothers and sisters, one by one. He strode up and down in front of the fireplace working himself into a frenzy. The fire roared and The Baron roared along with it. He took off his parka and flung it on the couch beside Nicky, who hadn't moved. As it landed beside Nicky's hand, a pistol slid out of one of the pockets; he recognized it as one of those from the display box he had seen in the den at the lodge. His mind raced. It was clear he wasn't going to be able to reason with The Baron. He had hoped things would be calm. He hadn't planned on violence. He became more and more incensed as The Baron continued to curse the members of the family. When he started in on Frederick, who Nicky remembered as the kindest person he had ever known, it was too much.

He grasped the pistol. It fit in his hand as easily as those he had carried on his flights in the Grasshopper. He stood and faced The Baron. He flicked off the safety, aimed at The Baron's chest and fired. Once. Twice. The Baron crumpled to the floor.

It was over. Or was it just beginning? Whichever, it couldn't be changed now. A thin trickle of blood began to trail across the floor. The Baron didn't move.

Nicky's love of airplanes and flying never abated. When he and Jane lived in England, he applied for a pilot's license under his new name. It was a long time coming, the whole process being wound up in enough red tape to rival that common to similar procedures in the United States. In addition to putting him in the air again, the license did much to establish his identity as Colin Taylor.

Their immigration to the United States grounded him again. However, he relentlessly assaulted the bureaucratic maze in quest of a pilot's license in his old country and won out in the end. Flying over the countryside of Pennsylvania reminded him of the Catskills and it was those flights that stirred the first longings to see the hills of home once again.

He became familiar with the area surrounding the small local airport where he flew on most weekends. He was intrigued by one farm about twenty miles away. The fence around one of its fields enclosed a long, narrow piece of flat ground that looked suspiciously like a landing strip. At one end stood an old barn facing the field with wide doors that seemed unusual for a barn. Something resembling a ragged windsock hung from a broken pole on the peak of the roof. He decided to investigate and one Sunday he and Jane drove out to the farm.

A tall, thin, white-haired man in his early seventies sat on the porch of the farmhouse, rocking back and forth in an old rocking chair as they stopped out front. When they went up the walk toward the porch, they caught the pleasant smell of a chicken dinner being prepared in the kitchen. it was difficult at first to explain to the man and his wife, who soon joined him on the porch, why they were there. But when Nicky told of his lifelong interest in flying and said he thought the barn out back looked more like an airplane hanger than a barn, the farmer's eyes lit up like landing lights on a dark night.

"Would you like to see what's in that hanger?" the old fellow chuckled.

No one could have been more surprised than Nicky when the hanger doors (it was a hanger, after all) were opened to reveal an old biplane covered with blankets. He was quick to recognize that it was a Spad XIII, a relic from the World War I battlefields of France.

"I ain't had her in the air for about twenty years, but she was a grand flier when last I did. Flew one just like her in the big war," the old-timer said proudly.

That was the beginning of many busy and pleasant weekends. Between Nicky and Jane; the farmer who, it turned out, had flown in the 27th Aero Squadron with Frank Luke, the Balloon Buster; and a young lad from the farm next door, who knew more about engines than any two other mechanics; they rebuilt the old 'plane. To commemorate the farmer's past, they restored it in the colors and markings of the old 27th, complete with the squadron's "screaming eagle" insignia and vertical stripes of red, white, and blue on the tail rudder.

It was a great day when Nicky took the Spad up on her maiden flight—well, maiden flight, second time around, that is. The farmer mowed the old landing strip and they put up a new pole and windsock on the roof of the barn. They painted the barn a bright red. Nicky could see it from afar off when he returned from a flight—it stood out like a beacon beckoning the 'plane home.

Most of Nicky's flights were of one- or two-hour duration. But in the early summer of 1965, he began to work out a flight plan for a week-long grand tour around the Northeast for early September. He didn't tell Jane, but the most important leg of the circuit was a pass up the valley of the Indian on the afternoon of the Sunday before Labor Day. And that's where he was at that appointed place and time.

He banked the Spad over Milltown and headed southeast up Indian Brook flying into the horseshoe of mountains that formed the valley. The road wound along the side of the stream and he easily picked out the sharp bend of Hemlock Turn. Off in the distance, he could see the pond as the sun reflected from its surface. Would they be there, he wondered? Had things changed? Had better times, old times, returned to those he loved—and missed?

He dipped the airplane low over the pond and saw the summer-house and the wide lawn. People were there, lots of people. He couldn't distinguish one from another, but he had no doubt who they were. He circled the pond and watched them as they watched him. Tears came to his eyes. How he wished he could land—even in the limbs of the old spruce tree—and see each of them up close.

But it was not to be. He put the Spad into a slow climb, turning for the gap between Twin and Indian mountains. He looked back over the tail of the 'plane as he cleared the ridge; back down the long valley of the Indian. Yes, he decided, yes, although a man was dead, it had been worthwhile.

13.
Sunday, September 5, 1965;
Friday, September 17, 1965

"SHADES OF THE PAST," said The Mouse. And that did it. Something about that darned cabin had bothered Ward Eastman for months. Often, he pictured it in his mind and searched again, looking for something he knew was there but couldn't quite see. Whatever it was seemed always just out of view. Something kept eluding him. Now a chance phrase had widened his field of vision, so to speak, and he saw what it was. He knew who had shot The Baron.

Everyone—himself included—had assumed (Jumped to the conclusion was more like it.) the reason The Baron had crawled to the back window and, with the last breaths of his life, pulled down the window shade was because he thought he heard someone at the back of the cabin. If someone was out there, they would have heard the noise of the shade falling, looked through the window, realized The Baron needed help, and gone to his aid. Or, so they all had thought. But that really didn't make much sense now that Ward looked at it differently. After all, the drapes at the large front windows had been opened wide—if someone had been outside the cabin, they would more likely have peered in those bright windows rather than through a little back window that looked in at a dark corner of the large room.

No, it was obvious now. The business with the window shade was The Baron's attempt to name his killer. He's a ghost—the shade of a dead person—The Baron was saying to those who would find his body. But The Baron's message was too subtle and they all misread it. Until now, that is. If the killer was a shade or a phantom, he had to be someone they all thought was dead. That was no puzzle; the only one thought dead in the whole cast of characters was Nicholas, the second-oldest Borden brother. His body hadn't been found and he wasn't declared dead by the government, only missing. Well, he wasn't just missing anymore. While Ward wasn't a betting man, he was ready to wager a goodly sum that the pilot of that old World War I airplane had been Nicholas Borden. Not only was the 'plane a shade of the past as The Mouse had said, if Ward was correct, then, so was the pilot. If Ward could find the airplane, he would probably find the murderer.

It wasn't until the middle of the second week following that Ward found enough spare time to make the trip across the Hudson River to Rhinebeck. Although he hadn't been there before, he had read an article in an area magazine about the old-time aerodrome Cole Palen had created on an abandoned farm just north of the historic village. The writer reported that Palen's collection consisted of airplanes of World War I vintage and earlier. Ward thought the 'plane they had seen might have come from this early field or, maybe, was one of those in Palen's living museum.

Not many people were around the aerodrome; no one seemed to be in charge. A couple of 'planes were parked along the edge of the landing strip while others could be seen in the old barns that had been converted to makeshift hangers. However, none of these airplanes had the markings of the one that had flown up the valley. In the open door of one of the hangers, Ward noticed a man standing on a stepladder working on the motor of an airplane.

Approaching the man and getting his attention, Ward asked, "Anyone here I can talk to about an old biplane I saw flying over the Catskills a couple of weeks ago?"

"Guess I'm as good as any," the man replied, wiping his greasy hands on the cloth that hung out of his back pocket. "Cole isn't here right now and won't be back until evening. I'm Clyde, kind of the mechanic, among other things, around here."

Ward described the old airplane, its colors and markings and, as he did, Clyde's face brightened. "Oh, the Spad. Wasn't she a beauty? That guy had done some job getting her in shape. The motor purred like a kitten. I looked it over for him while he was here. Told him it didn't need any help from me."

"Do you know who the pilot was? Or where he came from?" Ward inquired.

"Came from some place in Pennsylvania. Can't tell you exactly where. He stopped here to gas up. Name was Trainor or Taylor. Something like that. Cole took it all down because he was real interested in the 'plane. Fellow didn't want to sell though. Can't blame him. If that 'plane was mine, I wouldn't want to sell her either. Cole's here most days. Stop in again and I'm sure he'll be glad to talk to you."

Ward thanked Clyde for his good help and said he would come another day to see Palen. At least, he now knew Nicholas Borden was using another name and where he could find out his address. All that wasn't of real importance to Ward though; it was Burgin who would need that information so he could track down The Baron's killer.

It was a couple of days later when Ward, on his way to the Borden property, stopped in at the barracks in Milltown. Burgin was there, just getting into his car as Ward pulled into the parking lot. He waited by the car until Ward parked the pickup truck and then greeted him. "Hi, Eastman. It's been awhile. How've you been?"

Ward asked if they could talk as he had some interesting information about the Borden shooting. "Sure," Burgin replied. "I'm on my way to Albany to a meeting, but I have a few minutes. What have you got?"

"I think I know who shot Barron Borden." Ward paused so that could sink in. "It was his half-brother, Nicholas."

"My gawd, Eastman," Burgin laughed. "Where'd you ever come up with that cock-eyed idea? That guy's been dead for ten or twelve years. We checked into that. You know, Eastman, I always thought you were the best surveyor around these mountains and I respect you for that. However, surveying and tracking down killers are two different things. We do appreciate all the help you gave us back when this happened and for finding the murder weapon and all. But from now on, why don't you stick to surveying and we'll stick to running down criminals. Sorry to leave you so sudden, but I'm going to be late now. Drop by again when I've got more time to talk." With that,

Burgin got in his car and drove off out of the parking lot and down Route 28.

Ward was left standing by his truck, alone in the parking lot. It was evident that he and his information weren't wanted in this—or, probably, any other—investigation. Well, if that's the way it was, that's the way it would be, he vowed. As far as he was concerned, the police could search out their own evidence from now on.

Still, it was hard to just abandon the leads he had followed and difficult to blot out all the thoughts he had about the murder and the events surrounding it. He drove to the end of the town road up Indian Brook and parked the pickup there. He still had a key to the gate and the road beyond was dry, but he decided to walk up the valley. Maybe it would do him good. The quiet of the woods, the warmth of the late summer sun, and the colors of the leaves that were starting to change might calm the upset he was feeling.

Some of the lines to partition the property were further up the valley. He wanted to take another look at the lay of the land there before deciding where to put them so they would best conform to the family member's thoughts about dividing the lands of the estate. He did feel better when he reached the cabin; he was glad he had walked. He sat down on the rock in back of the cabin and lit his pipe.

This was where it had all started, he reflected. It really didn't seem that almost a year had passed since they found the body. Burgin was probably right. He was a better land surveyor than a detective. Still, the talents of one were similar to the other. He considered the character of old rail fences, piles of stones, tree blazes, and other physical evidence as a guide in determining where boundary lines and property corners should be located. It was the same as looking at the character of the evidence found in the investigation of a crime. And, by golly, that window shade had character.

He realized his pipe had gone out. He tamped down the tobacco in the bowl and lit it again. The Baron wasn't trying to signal for help by pulling down that shade. He had too little life left by that time to think about prolonging it. He was trying to leave a message—Ward was sure of it.

It was a lot like reading a deed. He always remembered a dictum he had read years ago in a land surveying textbook. He couldn't quote it exactly, but he never forgot the point it made.

In order to properly interpret a deed, the surveyor must put himself in the place of the scrivener, pick up the deed by the four corners, and read it.

And that's just what he had done here. He had put himself in the place of The Baron. Knowing The Baron's personality, Ward was sure the one thing he would want to do before he died was get revenge by telling who had shot him. So he turned to the only thing available to accomplish it. He pulled down the window shade. That was the deed he wrote. It had taken Ward ten months to get hold of all four corners of it, but now that he finally had, he was able to read it.

Ward knew his reasoning was a bit nebulous and that those who didn't think the way land surveyors did would have trouble reconciling with his conclusion. But then he was reminded of another axiom. It was Sherlock Holmes who preached this one.

It is an old maxim of mine that when you have excluded the impossible, whatever remains, however improbable, must be the truth.

It certainly was improbable that Nicholas Borden was the murderer, but it was the only solution that remained. According to Holmes, then, it "must be the truth."

His pipe was really out this time. Ward tapped it against the rock, clearing the bowl of the now-cold ashes. Time to get to work, he ordered himself. The murder investigation was over as far as he was concerned. He knew who the murderer was and where he could be found. If no one else cared, so be it.

However, a bevy of questions still nagged at him. Did any of the family know Nicky was alive? If they did, did they know it before the murder or after? If before, were they accessories before the fact? If after, were they accessories after the fact? When The Mouse said, "Shades of the past," did she mean the airplane or the pilot? And how come on the day of the murder, every member of the family was conveniently such a long distance away from the valley and all with unshakable alibis? Had the murder actually been a conspiracy with all of them involved?

But those questions were no longer Ward Eastman's to answer, if they ever were. Still, the way the property was being partitioned was certainly curious. Jen was to get land at the lower end of the valley, so that her share would adjoin the old Kirk place where she and Amos lived. The Mouse was to be next up the valley, where that nice, little, yellow house was. Linc selected the land southwesterly from the road, including the lodge, and that was certainly his right, being the oldest son of the oldest son and all that. Jack was to get the land northeasterly of the road and opposite Linc's part. But, why was there to be a fifth share? Why was the remote land at the head of the valley, including the cabin, set out as a separate section with no name attached to it?

Ward Eastman really wondered about that. However, it was none of his business; he was just a land surveyor. He turned his back on the cabin and moved off up the mountain.

Author's Note

OVER THE YEARS OF MY CAREER, it has been my good fortune to work in a profession that sent me off to climb the high hills of the Catskills, to wade their cold streams, to stand on their snowy and wind-blown summits, and to visit remote places deep in their cloves and vales where few people have been. The greatest reward of these experiences is the images retained in my mind of the sights, sounds, and smells of these times of my life. I have drawn on these images to set the stage for some of the scenes in the preceding narrative. They have been taken at random from various sites throughout the Catskills and are not really located in a single valley as the text might lead one to believe.

The reader, if at all familiar with the Catskills, will recognize some actual places, villages, streams, and roads. Many, however, are fictitious.

Some will wonder about the stream acquisitions mentioned in some detail in the story. I have been privileged to survey some rather extensive properties in various valleys and hollows that enclose some of the now-historic Catskills' trout streams. The type of strip acquisition described is not unusual along these waters. In fact, some of the quoted deed language in the narrative is taken from the actual deeds to some of these strips of land and water.

Except for a couple of minor characters, the people in this book are fictional. A few readers will be sure they recognize some of the others. If they do, it's by chance only, not by my design. A few of the names used are real, but where I have cited such names, the actual people have passed from this world. For instance, Frank Borden and Byron Hill really were forest rangers back in the beginning days of my career. They—and many others—gave much encouragement to this (then) young, neophyte woodsman who had much to learn. I write their names with respect and in remembrance of them and their fellows. The taxpayers of New York State got their money's worth when that old guard was standing the watch.

The names of some of the old-time surveyors mentioned are real as are the dates of their surveys. However, the lines they ran back in those bygone days don't always fit on the ground as I describe them. I am a better land surveyor than this shifting around of old lines would indicate.

The names of some of the mountain peaks in the story are real and others are not. The fictional ones are those in and around where the main action occurs. This is so the site of the murder and the property on which it takes place will be entirely imaginary. But the Catskill Mountains are real and I wouldn't have it any other way.

Other Ward Eastman mysteries you will enjoy:

Murder in the Catskills

Ward Eastman finds a skeleton in rugged terrain near the hamlet of South Branch. From the moment he starts to unravel his first mystery, Eastman finds himself enmeshed amid layers of genealogy, history, and topography.

Mischief in the Catskills

A deer hunter is lost in a blinding blizzard. Eastman and his surveying crew are joined by law enforcement officials and volunteers as the search intensifies. But was the hunter really lost? A mystery novella with five masterful short stories.

Murder in the Shawangunks

A surveyor in the small, very old mountain range between the Catskills and the Hudson River had been found at the base of one of its craggy cliffs. His death was ruled accidental, but Ward Eastman, tracing his lines main years later, had different ideas.

About the author

Norman J. Van Valkenburgh was born in West Kill in Greene County and has spent most of his life in or in sight of the Catskill Mountains. He is a licensed surveyor and 32-year veteran of the New York State Department of Environmental Conservation.

About the publisher

Purple Mountain Press, founded in 1973, is a publishing company committed to producing the best original books of regional interest as well as bringing back into print significant older works. For a free catalog of more than 300 hard-to-find books about New York State, write Purple Mountain Press, Ltd., P.O. Box 309, Fleischmanns, New York 12430-0378, or call 914-254-4062, or fax 914-254-4476, or email Purple@catskill.net. Website: http://www.catskill.net/purple